2

THE CAMEO SERIES

The Honeymoon House

GRACE LIVINGSTON HILL

Tyndale House
Publishers, Inc.
Wheaton, Illinois

These stories were originally published by
the J. B. Lippincott Company in 1938.

First printing, August 1984

Library of Congress Catalog Card Number 84-50539
ISBN 0-8423-1476-8
Copyright © 1984 by Robert L. Munce Publishing Co.
All rights reserved
Printed in the United States of America

CONTENTS

THE HONEYMOON HOUSE

I go to prepare a place for you ... I will come again and receive you unto myself. JOHN 14:2, 3.

ANGELA was lovely, there was no denying that. When she glanced up from her drawing and her clear eyes looked straight into yours from under those level pleasant brows, you did not wonder at the gorgeous diamond she wore upon the third finger of her left hand. She seemed altogether lovely and greatly to be desired.

She had delicate features and rich dark hair that curled away from her white forehead entrancingly. She had a ravishing smile and a look of character about her whole sweet being. Those who watched her daily admired and loved her greatly and felt that the man whose promised wife she was had a rare future before him.

She sat at her work in the bay window where a glint of light touched the waves of her lovely hair, and brought out the delicate coloring of her rounded cheek and the clear light in her eyes. Her friend Ellen, entering, paused to take in the picture and put it away in her memory as a precious treasure.

"Good morning, Angela," she said as the girl looked up, her pencil poised for another skillful line in her drawing. "You're just a picture as you sit there. I wish I had my camera with me. I'd like to have that expression to keep. I'd like to make a copy and send it to David. I know he'd love it!"

Angela smiled indulgently. "You are a dear old flatterer," she said, "and David has already more pictures of me than he knows what to do with. It isn't really necessary for him to have another. Sit down, won't you? Excuse me for going right on working; I must finish this drawing and get it in the late morning mail. But I would love to have you stay and talk to me while I work."

"Well, then, tell me the news! When is David coming back?"

Angela smiled contentedly. "Oh, sometime, I suppose. He doesn't say just when."

"But aren't you awfully impatient to see him? I don't see how you can possibly stand this long separation. He was always so devoted."

Angela smiled. "I'm pretty busy, you know," she said, with a proud little lift of her head. "I'm getting ready to earn my living, and I'm doing quite well, they tell me. I've even got a few orders of my own. This is an order I'm working on now. Of course I haven't finished my apprenticeship yet in the office, but they are letting me do a few little things on the side for people who don't want to pay the head architect and the head decorator's prices. See what I'm doing. Isn't this going to be the prettiest room? It's a great ugly square room we're making over, in a country house. See this bay window! Isn't that delightful? And I'm putting a seat all around it upholstered in blue velour. There's a wonderful rug for the floor, the loveliest old Chinese blue, and the furniture is perfect; rare old specimens. I picked them up cheap here and there—at least, I got a price on them, and I think the owner will take them when he sees this picture. I'm so enthusiastic about my work, and it's such fun to earn my own money!"

"It's lovely," said the friend, looking over Angela's shoulder, "but—what will you do with it all when you are married?"

"Married?" Angela lifted sweet eyes vaguely. "Oh, that's a long time off yet! I haven't thought much about that. Of course that will come sometime, but just now my business is to succeed and begin earning my own living. I'm here, and David is away. My main thought has to be put on my work right here and now."

"But David was so impatient to be married."

"Well, he is, I guess," said Angela. "But we can't be married till he gets back, you know, and why should I just sit around and harp on that when I can't do a thing about it?"

"But isn't he succeeding in what he went to do?" asked the friend, puzzled.

"Oh, yes, I think he is. I haven't had time to write very long letters, and I haven't asked him much about it, but he seems satisfied with his work."

"But doesn't he say a word about when he will be done and be coming back?"

"Oh, yes, now and then. But he doesn't say when. Several times he has said he might surprise me someday. The last letter, I believe, said it might be soon!"

"Why, he might be coming today!" exclaimed the friend.

"Oh, I hardly think so!" Angela smiled contentedly.

"But I should think you'd be so thrilled about it you couldn't do a thing!" said the friend, looking at her calm face wonderingly.

"Why should I get thrilled about something that I don't know a thing about?" said the girl pleasantly. "Time enough to get thrilled when it happens—*if* it happens. You know, I never wanted him to go away at all. I wanted him to stay right here and get into business in this part of the world and begin to be a success. But no, he had to run away to the other side of the world, and I just couldn't understand it. So I got to work to improve myself, and improve the time while I was waiting."

"But aren't you writing all the time to beg him to come at once?"

"Why, no, it doesn't seem quite nice to talk about it."

"But I should think you just couldn't stand being separated so long. He's such a wonderful man!"

"Yes, he is rather wonderful, isn't he?" said Angela calmly. "But I'm not worrying. He's doing his work and I'm doing mine. I really couldn't spare much time to go about with him just now, if he *were* here. I want to succeed. In the end he'll come, of course, but I hope by that time to have reached my ambition. Do you know what I want to do? I want to build a house for us to live in! I want to build it all myself, and furnish it before he gets here, and I want to have reached the place where I am self-supporting!"

"Oh, but do you think he would like that?" asked her friend, astonished. "I think a man always wants to feel he can take care of his wife."

"Oh, that's the old-fashioned way of looking at things, of course, but I shouldn't like to have to depend on somebody else for everything. I'd rather earn my own money and my own position in life."

"But David would be grieved, I'm sure," said the friend. "I remember hearing him tell my mother how happy he was going to be, providing for you as a lady should be provided for. I remember his look when he said it; a kind of light seemed to glow all over his face as if it came from within. 'She shall have the best that is to be had!' he said with a great tenderness in his voice. 'It is going to be my delight to work for her and get her all that she wants.' "

"Oh, yes, he's very sweet," said Angela easily. "He writes that way sometimes, too. But I feel a girl is much more independent when she has an income and a business of her own. Her husband respects her more, and they get on better."

"But Angela, dear, not a *house!* You wouldn't try to build the house that you two are to live in! Build a house *for sale*, perhaps, but not the house you will go to as a bride. It would hurt him. I'm sure it would hurt him."

"Oh, no, not when he sees the house. It's going to be the darlingest little nest of a place, and yet spacious too, and with all the loveliest contrivances for comfort and beauty. You see, no man understands what kind of a house a girl wants, and if I get it all fixed up before he comes, why, he's sure to like it, and there won't be any difficulty about details."

"But, my dear, how do you know he will be willing to settle where you build your house?"

"That's just it. I want to make it impossible to go away from my business. I'm expecting to have established a big business by the time he comes, a business that will be really worthwhile. I don't intend to run any risks of having to leave it. If the business is here and the house is here all ready for a home, he couldn't help but like it."

"Oh, Angela dear, I'm afraid you are making trouble for yourself. No man likes his bride to get the home ready. That is *his* place."

"But David loves me, you know." Angela smiled with calm assurance, making a neat little picture of a chair with her sharp pencil point in the room she was building.

There was silence for a moment while her friend tried to think how to make it plain to her.

"But hasn't *he* said anything about the details of your home, where it shall be, and what kind of a house he means to prepare for you?"

"Oh, yes, I believe he has mentioned such things once or twice. But I usually save his letters to read at night just before I go to bed, and sometimes, to tell you the truth, I'm so worn out with the work of the day that I don't always read them through. I fall asleep."

"You don't read his letters through!" said Ellen aghast. "The letters of a lover like that?"

"Oh, I generally read most of them. When I have time I read them through. They really are lovely letters. His diction is exquisite sometimes. It reads just like poetry. But when one is hard at work on practical things it is often difficult to get into the clouds and read dreams of loveliness."

"Oh, Angela!" protested her friend. "You don't realize how wonderful it is to have a lover who takes time to write you long letters and tell you all his beautiful poetic dreams for you."

"Oh, I write to him every day myself, of course," said Angela a bit haughtily, as one would say, "I always say my prayers." "You know I am as busy as he is, and he ought to be glad I take time to write."

Angela's friend gave her a strange, half-pitying look.

"What do you write about?" she said softly.

"Oh, I write about my work. I tell him every little detail. I try to make him appreciate the color schemes I am working out in the rooms I decorate, and the symmetry of line in the buildings I draw. You see, I want him to understand and appreciate the loveliness of the house I have built, when I get it done. And so I keep him in touch with my own progress. I want him to know how well I am doing, so that he will appreciate me too, you know, and see how I am working to prepare this home in my native land."

Angela paused to make it plain on her drawing where the windows were located and which way the doors swung, before she went on again.

"Writing letters like that serves two purposes," she said. "It counts as a letter to David, and it serves to keep clear in my mind all that I have accomplished during the day. It is excellent discipline for the mind. And he cannot fail to see what a helper he is getting in marrying me, someday."

"But when is that day to be, dear?" asked her friend again. "Aren't you eager for its coming?"

"Oh, so-so!" said Angela with a ripple of laughter. "I'm having a grand time. I love my work and I want to get on. I'm earning real money and putting it where it will tell for the most! And evenings now and then I have a wonderful time with some of my friends."

"But don't you ever feel sad when you see the other girls with their fiancés, to think yours is so far away?"

"Oh, there are always plenty of men who are willing to show me a good time if I can spare an evening," said Angela carelessly. "I went out with Herbert Boone last night to a party. We had a wonderful evening with the old crowd, and stayed out so late that I'm really sleepy today in consequence."

"Herbert Boone? Why, Angela! I thought he was a bitter enemy of David. I thought he had once threatened David's life."

"Oh, well, one can't stop on little things like that.

Besides I only go with him occasionally."

"And does David know?"

"Why, really, I'm not sure whether I ever mentioned it to David or not."

"But, my dear, isn't that rather disloyal to David? His confessed enemy?"

"Oh, darling!" Angela laughed. "How old-fashioned you are! One doesn't stop to consider little differences between men friends when one goes out to have a good time of an evening! Really, darling, where have you been these last few years that you haven't seen that people have dropped that old code and choose their friends where they like? Why, Nan Lacey goes around quite a bit with the present wife of her former husband and nobody seems to mind."

"But a sworn enemy of your beloved, Angela, one who has tried to kill him on more than one occasion."

"I'm sure David wouldn't mind my doing it in the least," said Angela lightly. "He was always broadminded. And really, we behave so well that I wouldn't mind taking even David himself along with us. Anyway," with a toss of her head, "he can't mind what he doesn't see."

"But won't he feel it, dear? Those things are subtle, and they hurt."

"Well, *he* went away, didn't he? He left me here alone, didn't he? He can't expect me to sit and mope forever, can he?"

"Ah, but he went away to get ready to be with you always. He went away to prepare for you to be with him."

"That's all right when the time comes," said Angela with a light laugh. "I'm not married yet."

"But doesn't he give you any intimation how soon to expect him? Haven't you any guide as to what to expect?"

"Oh, yes, he talks a lot about it, but in such a strange way," said Angela with a bit of a frown. "Sometimes I can't make out what it is all about. He mixes up sort of fairy stories, about flowers and trees and rain. Once when I asked him how soon he was coming he talked about the fig tree budding. He speaks about the summer rain, and a prince from the North, and education, and new inventions, and all sorts of queer things. I can make nothing of it. Such fanciful language. Not long ago he wrote, 'We shall feed among the lilies,' and goodness knows I don't want to go camping! I have given up trying to understand him. You know he has been away since before my father and mother died, and has been talking about coming back ever since. But he hasn't come yet. I don't think he means to come for a long, long time, and I'm just as well satisfied, for I want to get on in the world before he comes."

"And yet you are wearing his ring on your finger."

"Oh, yes, we are engaged!" said Angela with a bright smile.

"And you love him still, Angela?"

"Why, yes, of course I'm fond of him," said Angela a bit crossly.

"I wonder if you remember him well, dear?"

"Of course I do, and if I didn't he is always sending me pictures. I couldn't forget him."

"Pictures? You mean photographs?"

"Yes, photographs and snapshots. He seems to want me to keep in close touch with him, but he doesn't in the least realize how busy I am. Sometimes I don't have time to open the pictures for days. Now that I think of it, one came yesterday, and I haven't opened it yet. I just couldn't stop. This drawing has to be in the mail this morning."

"I'm hindering you!" said her friend self-reproachfully.

"Not a bit," said the girl, writing her name with a tiny flourish at the bottom of the drawing. "I'm all done now. I've only to put this in the mailing tube and address it, and then I'm at leisure for the rest of the day. I'm glad you came in."

"But aren't you going to open your picture, Angela? I'd like to see how David looks now. That is, if you don't mind my seeing it right off. Perhaps you want it all to yourself the first day or two, and if so I won't intrude."

"Oh, mercy no! I'm not sentimental like that. Here, I'll give you the package and you can open it while I address this."

"But you oughtn't to do that!" protested the friend. "Think how he would feel if he knew that you had let another open the package that he did up for your eye to see first."

"Nonsense! That's ridiculous. Open it, please! I may forget it for another week if you don't."

There was silence while Angela wrote, and the friend cut the string and unwrapped the picture.

"Ah!" she said, and was still again. "It is David! I would have known him anywhere. And yet, he seems older, somehow sadder!"

"Sad?" said Angela offendedly. "What has he to be sad about?"

She came and stood by her friend and looked at the picture over her shoulder.

"I wouldn't be expected to know," said the friend.

"Well, he certainly has everything his own way!" said Angela. "He went away in spite of all that I could do, and he seems to be staying as long as he pleases. I don't see why he should be sad."

"Is he sure of you, Angela?"

"Sure of *me?*" said Angela, now thoroughly annoyed. "What has that to do with being sad?"

"If you are his, and he isn't sure of your love, then there would be good reason."

"Goodness, how silly you are! Silly and sentimental! David and I fully understand each other, so you needn't get any such notions."

There was another long silence while the two looked at the picture.

"I don't like the way his hair is cut!" said Angela in a cross voice. "I'll have to write to him about that. It's most unbecoming. I like to have things beautiful. He used to be so handsome."

There was another silence, and then the friend spoke quietly, almost as if she were speaking to herself.

"And that is *the scar!*" she said sorrowfully. "The same scar. It shows yet!"

"*Scar?*" said Angela, leaning over to look closer. "I never noticed a scar in his pictures before. I guess he usually has the other side of his face taken. But what scar do you mean? He didn't have any scar that I saw when he went away."

"The scar he got when he saved you from the fire!"

"Did he get his face scarred then? I didn't know it! I was sick, you know, for a long time; and before I got up he went away. He only came at night to say good-bye. That was when he put this ring on my finger."

"Yes, he was scarred very badly on one side of his face. But the doctors grafted on skin. I understood it was healing, but it seems to show in the picture."

"Oh, I don't think that is a scar at all! It is just a blemish in the picture. I wouldn't like to think he got scarred saving me. I'm sure it was utterly unnecessary. He always did insist on doing unnecessary things for me, when I could perfectly well do them for myself. I'm sure I could have walked out of a burning building as well as he did, if he hadn't picked me up and made it impossible."

"My dear, you were unconscious! Yes, he found you lying in a room that was all aflame! You were as good as dead when he struggled away from the firemen who were trying to prevent his going back to find you. He went through smoke and flame, and found you lying unconscious on the floor. A moment after he started down the stairs with you in his arms the ceiling of that room fell! And the floor fell through to the next story below. How he ever got you down those stairs nobody ever knew, but he accomplished it, at this price!" and she pointed to the scar.

"Oh, I'm quite sure you are mistaken!" said Angela pertly. "Such things are always exaggerated afterward, and it's a long time ago. I suppose people have talked in town and made a lot of it."

"Didn't David ever tell you about it?"

"No, I never encouraged him to. I was too upset before he went away, and when he wrote and mentioned anything about the fire I just skipped that. I hate gruesome stories!"

"Oh, but Angela, he loved you! And he saved you! And he'll surely come back to you."

"Yes, I suppose so," said Angela, twisting her gorgeous ring about her finger, "but somehow I cannot make it seem real anymore."

"But suppose he should be coming tomorrow, or even tonight, dear?"

Angela laughed.

"He wouldn't come like that. He's been away a long time. He's not any more likely to come tomorrow than he was to come all of the yesterdays."

"But he might have come then. Were you ready to meet him?"

"Well, no, frankly, there's a lot I want to do before I leave home."

"But oughtn't you to get ready? If you're going to be with him the other things that you might do wouldn't matter, would they? If I were you I'd get everything ready."

"Ready?" Angela laughed. "*Ready!* According to

him I don't need to do a thing. What do you think that absurd man wrote me a few days ago? He said I wouldn't need to prepare a wedding dress. He said he was going to *bring* me one when he came! *Imagine* it! Being married in a dress *a man* had selected! I wrote and told him nothing doing! I told him I preferred to select my own wedding dress!"

"Oh, Angela! How could you! Don't you know that's the old oriental custom for the bridegroom to give the bride her outfit? He meant it for a delicate attention. It has a wonderfully sweet meaning."

"Delicate attention indeed!" sneered Angela, making her lips look as unpleasant as such beautiful lips could look. "I'm not an oriental, and this is the modern world. I prefer the customs of today!"

"Oh, but Angela, you don't understand him. You are hurting him! My dear, I wish you would write and tell him you are glad he has done such a lovely thing. I know you will be glad you did it. I just feel it is something lovely! I knew him years ago and he has a very beautiful soul. You would be glad, I know, if you did it."

Angela's eyes suddenly flashed fire and her straight placid brows grew stormy.

"*Really!*" she said haughtily. "I do wish you would mind your own business! I can't see why you think you have any right to pry into mine, and then offer suggestions! It is *I* who am engaged to David, not you. And I shall conduct my own affairs as I see best."

"I'm sorry," said the friend, rising and brushing away the tears from her eyes. "I love you both and it has been so wonderful to think of you loving each other. I can't bear to see such an ideal companionship hurt in any way. I only thought, what if he should come and you not be ready for him! It would be so dreadful for him to come and find you out enjoying yourself with his enemy."

Angela laughed.

"Spare yourself," she said disagreeably. "He has no idea of coming at present, I am sure, and by the time he does come I'll very likely have attained my ambition and be ready to see him. Anyhow, he'll have learned a lot, and not be so sentimental."

"Angela, excuse me, dear, I must just say this. You know it isn't exactly sentiment, what a man feels for the one whose life he has saved. I was looking at your beautiful face this afternoon and thinking how it was his doing that you were not all scarred and dreadful for life instead of himself. Your beautiful face might have been a dead face if he hadn't risked his own life and manly beauty to save yours. You owe him your life and beauty, Angela, and you mustn't hurt him. If he brings you a wedding dress you must wear it and be glad, whatever it is."

Angela laughed.

"Even if it should be only white linen?" she queried comically. "That's what he says it is!"

"Yes, even if it should be white linen," said her friend solemnly. "Listen, Angela dear, I can't get away from the thought of you lying white and still on the cot in the firehouse, and David lying grimed and swathed in bandages on the floor not far away. His hands and feet wrapped in bandages, his face covered with bandages. Oh, Angela! How he loves you! Old Tim Morgan, the fire chief, told me once that the minute he came out of his swoon he asked for you, and when they said you were coming around all right, and were not scarred at all, he said 'Thank God!' and swooned away again! Angela, he loves you with a love that is worth all other treasures of earth. Be good to him, Angela, be persuaded—"

"Oh, for heaven's sake!" said Angela, now thoroughly angry. "Am I a babe in arms to be dictated to about my love affairs? Kindly change the subject, won't you? Come, I've got to go out and mail this drawing. Will you come with me? And for pity's sake, forget David and let's talk about my business career."

"But if he should come for you soon, Angela?" ventured the friend again.

"Well, there's no chance of his coming for a long time, if he comes at all," said Angela. "Come! Now let's be a little cheerful."

But after she had parted from her friend and turned back toward her home, she could not get away from the words Ellen had spoken about David. Somehow a picture of him as she had known him at first came back to her mind—handsome, bright, the most admired boy among her schoolmates. How proud she had been to have him choose her to walk with, carrying her schoolbooks, accompanying her everywhere. How gorgeous her diamond had seemed when he first put it upon her finger, before worldly ambition had taken root in her heart.

The picture of him was so vivid as he used to be in their school days that when she reached her room she took out the picture again and sat looking at it.

Yes, those were the same eyes that looked out at her, only the sparkle had gone out of them. She could see what her friend had meant by saying he looked sad. What had made him this way? Had she had anything to do with it?

She recalled how empty her letters had been of late, mere descriptions of the rooms she was creating for the notable decorators and architects for whom she was working. She had written over and over again about her own success. And letter by letter his own had grown more grave and sad, except for that lily-language toward the end, that talk of "my beloved in the garden" that she had not understood. It was as if she were very far away from him, separated by a thick veil.

Yet it had been his own doing that he had gone away. She picked up the picture that had fallen in her lap and studied it again. Was that a scar or had it been the mere imagination of her friend?

Yes, that was a scar! There was no mistaking it! Why had she not known it before? Could it be that she *had* been the cause of that scar? She could not bear the thought. The tears were gathering in her eyes in spite of all her resolves. She brushed them away fiercely and looked harder at the picture, which seemed to look back at her, steadily, sorrowfully. Was it also accusingly? Oh, could that be true?

Presently she could bear it no longer, and flinging the picture into a drawer out of sight she put on her hat and went down to the firehouse seeking the fire chief. She must know the truth of this, once and for all. Did she owe her life to David? Or was this all a fantasy of her friend's imagination?

The fire chief was embarrassed when the beautiful girl came seeking him. He had long watched her from afar and curled his lip at her indifference, at the ingratitude of a girl whose life had been saved at such fearful cost to her lover; she seemed to have forgotten him. But now he dropped his eyes before her loveliness and knew not what to say.

At last her pleading unlocked his grim old lips and he told her the story in detail, not sparing her. He even took a kind of pleasure in seeing her lips quiver, and her body wince as the story went on. David was to him a very great hero, and he did not spare description when it came to his sufferings in this girl's behalf. He had visited him in the hospital. He had himself taken David, at his own insistence, to visit Angela that night before he left for a foreign land where he had business. He knew how unfit David had been to make that farewell call. He knew what it had cost him to go the jeweler's and select that diamond, what pain he endured when he came to say good-bye. And when Angela left the firehouse she knew all about it too.

She went back to her beautifully appointed suite of rooms where she worked, and took his picture out again. She took out all the pictures that he had sent her, to try and piece the story together. She studied the scar on his face which had suddenly grown wondrously dear, and she wept over it. Looking at his picture now, and knowing all that he had done for her, she began suddenly to see herself, as if a picture of her own petted life were there in the frame beside his. She saw the selfishness in her heart. She saw how she had treated him, and how she must have hurt him! Such love as his had been! She remembered how she had been dancing gaily through the days since he left, filled with her own ambitions, her own desire to reach the place in her chosen profession. She thought of her desire to design and execute the house of her dreams, and fill it with all the lovely things in which she delighted. She had scarcely had a thought of him from one week's end to another. Going out with other men, she had amused herself flirting with a world that was alien to all that he loved. Even seeking pleasure with his enemy!

All this she saw and bowed her head in shame and wept again. Ah! Such love! And such unforgivable scorn and indifference as she had given in return! He would not love her now if he knew what she really was, what she had become since he had gone away!

Then suddenly she was seized with a great desire to read his letters over again, every one from the beginning. It would be torture to her soul, but she would read them. And then, somehow she must muster courage to confess her past disloyalty and indifference! She must return his gorgeous ring, that she had so loved to flaunt in the eyes of her world, that they might the more admire and worship *her*. She saw now that she had used his love simply to further her own ends.

So she began to read, and her heart was more and

more humiliated till her tears flowed so that she could scarcely see the written words.

There were many paragraphs which had not meant a thing to her when she had first read them so hastily. But now, in the light of what she knew he had done for her, their meaning was suddenly revealed, and her heart was thrilled with his great love and tenderness.

And then she came to the most humiliating letters of all. Those she had not even opened. And lo, she found that he *knew all about her!* He had kept in touch with her movements from afar. He told her in those letters how he knew just what she had done; he knew all her selfishness and indifference and her disloyalty to him, and yet he said he loved her still! "With an *everlasting* love!" he said. He told her that he would forgive and *forget* what she had done! That he would put her disloyalty behind his back, he would drown her indifference in the depths of the sea, her selfishness and ambition and sin he would remember no more! He would put all those things "as far as the east is from the west." Because he had gone through death for her he would count these things as though she had never done them. Such love! It was unbelievable!

And she, what should she do? There was no longer need for her to confess her sins, for he already knew them. It only remained for her to acknowledge them.

But, yes, there was one more thing she could do! She could own to him that now she really loved him. Too late for her to win his admiration and respect, of course. Too late for him to see in her all that a bridegroom had a right to see in his bride. But even so, at last she had found out her mistake, and her punishment was that she loved him with a love that burned through her shamed and humiliated soul like a sword thrust. So far as she was concerned, she was *his*, and his *forever*, now, whether he wanted her or not.

But now as she looked at the dates of these long-ago letters, and remembered that she had never answered them except by long accounts of her own works and ambitions, and by worldly requests for him to do something more for her, she began to feel that surely, since that letter of forgiveness, he must have cast her off forever! He had written her full pardon weeks ago, and she had not even so much as referred to it. If he knew that she had not even taken the trouble to read it, surely he would feel that that was unforgivable!

She looked at that latest picture again and now she saw the scar standing out clearly. Had he sent that to remind her how he had suffered for her? Ah, could she ever by a life's devotion make him believe that now she really loved him, as a bride should love?

She remembered that before he went away he had said that he was going to prepare a place for her. Shame covered her anew when she thought of her own ambitions to build a house in her own land that should be strong and enduring, and with but grudging room for him, and no thought whatever of the place he had been preparing for her. Did he know that too?

But while she thought upon all this her telephone

began to ring. At first she ignored it, for she would not be interrupted in this searching of her soul. But finally its insistence annoyed her and she reached out and took down the receiver.

"This is Western Union," said a voice. "A telegram! Will you take it now?"

Angela's heart almost stopped beating. Had something happened to David? How terrible if she was never able to tell him of her shame and sorrow! How terrible if she could never tell him how she loved him now, how all was changed, and how repentant she was. If David should be dead! If she could never thank him for bearing the scars for her!

The operator's voice came insistently: "Will you take the message now?"

She heard her own faltering voice saying yes, and then the operator again:

"Have prepared a mansion. Am on my way to get you. Be watching! I shall be there soon. There may be some delay, yet I *may* be there today! I love you.
                                                              David."

Then Angela's heart leaped with joy! He knew it all, and yet he loved her! He was coming soon! He had prepared a mansion! And he would be bringing her wedding dress!

Suddenly she sprang up. He had told her to watch! He might be coming any minute now! And there was a great deal for her to do before he came. Could she accomplish it all?

She gave not a thought to her life ambition, her careful drawing from which she had hoped to win a prize that would set her feet on the high road to success. She had forgotten it entirely. She was going home with her bridegroom to the mansion he had prepared for her. There was much to do, but not anything of her own devising. There were things that he had asked her to do before he went away. She had forgotten all about them in her absorption in herself. He had given her messages that he had asked her to deliver to some of his friends, and to people in whom he was interested—messages of hope and cheer and help to people in sorrow and distress—and she had not even remembered them until now.

Also he had asked her to look up some of his relatives who were to be invited to the wedding and get to know them before the wedding day. He wanted her to love them as he did. Oh, there was a great deal to be done and so little time in which to do it! How could he ever forgive her for her negligence of those he loved? Her carelessness about giving the help he had sent? So much to be done, and *perhaps* only the rest of this day in which to do it!

She arose hastily and prepared to go out on his errands, but as she was just ready to go, a caller came to see her about some work he wanted done. He was one of the great men of the earth. He had seen her drawings and had chosen her to do a huge building planned for amusement and entertainment, an operation that would be known throughout the country. The doing of it would place her beyond her highest ambitions in her world of business, and make her a success in her chosen line beyond anything she had ever hoped.

But she shook her head, scarcely pausing to realize the magnitude of what was being offered to her.

"I could not do your work," she said in a clear firm voice. "Circumstances have changed with me, and your work would involve a letting down of standards that have suddenly become dear to me. Besides, I have no time. I am soon to be married, and I have a great deal to do. I shall have to decline your proposition."

As she turned from seeing her caller out, she noticed lying on a little table by the door a card with a newspaper clipping, a bit of a poem, pasted on it, and Ellen's name penciled below. "Dear Ellen! She must have come and left it here while I went to the firehouse!" She read the poem, her heart strangely stirred.

The angels from their thrones on high
Look down on us with wondering eye,
That where we are but passing guests
We build such strong and solid nests,
And where we hope to stay for aye
We scarce take pains one stone to lay!

Like a knife the little rhyme went through her heart. Ah! That was what she had been doing, building a house *here* for her*self*, when a mansion was being prepared for her in another country! And Ellen had seen her disloyalty, and had taken this quiet gentle way of trying to make her see what she was doing! Dear Ellen!

Suddenly she stepped over to the table in the window where lay all the blueprints and plans for the house she had meant to build, and with one motion of her arm she swept them all into the wastebasket! What were they to her now? She was going home with her bridegroom to dwell in the mansion he had prepared for her, and it would be far more perfect than any she could have designed for herself, because he had made it for her! Because he loved her! He had bought her life with his scarred face, his wounded hands and feet, even his shed blood!

She shuddered as she remembered the words of the fire chief.

Then with a swift bright look around the room, with all its careful appointments—the room that now seemed so transient and imperfect in the thought of the mansion she was soon to see—she went out to do her lord's bidding, for he had told her to watch and be ready for his coming, which might perhaps be today!

LIFE OUT OF
DEATH

AFTERWARD Philip Gardley remembered his brother Stephen as he stood at the curb just a minute before it happened. What a pleasant smile had been on his face, and how tall and straight and handsome he had looked! The memory wrenched Philip's heart with a dull never-ceasing pain. Stephen had always been such a wonderful brother, more like a father than a brother to Philip, who could not remember his father.

It happened just after the brothers had completed an important conference arranging for Philip to enter into full partnership in the business which Stephen had built up into phenomenal prominence and success. Philip had finished a leisurely college education, topping it off with a prolonged European trip. They came out of the house together to drive down to the office in Stephen's car, which stood in front of their home. And Philip, seeing a girl across the street, called a greeting to her. He stepped out into the road the better to hear what she was saying, his Panama hat in hand, a smile on his lips, the honors of the partnership in the business resting lightly upon his irresponsible shoulders.

He glanced back as he stepped out into the road and caught that last glimpse of his brother standing on the curb with that look of quiet satisfaction upon his face, as if the thing he had just done meant the summit of his desire.

Even as Philip called out: "Just a minute, Steve," the idea touched the back of his mind a bit superficially: "Good old Steve! I believe this partnership means more to him than it does to me! He always was an unselfish fellow. I must buck up and take things more seriously!" He flung an easy smile behind him, and caught that last vivid impression.

Afterward nobody could describe how it happened. The street was broad and smooth, with plenty of room everywhere. There was no one in sight either way as Philip stepped out. An instant later a low-bodied, speedy sport car careened around the corner on two wheels and whirled madly toward him. Its twelve cylinders merely purred in the distance, and as it shot forward it gave no warning, sounded no horn. Only Stephen, standing on the curb, saw the onrushing danger. He gave one lunge forward and pushed his brother out of the way, but was struck himself and crushed by the heavy car as it sped wildly on and vanished around the next corner, its low-crouched driver taking no time to look back.

The girl across the street screamed and covered

her face with her hands. Philip, unaware of what had really happened, bruised and much shaken, highly indignant, gathered himself up to look toward that gallant figure of the brother who had stood smiling just a moment before, and found him gone! And down in the road at his feet lay a mangled, limp form with blood streaming from the face.

A crowd began to gather. The frightened mother rushed from the house and knelt in the road beside her son. Someone sent for the police and another sent for the ambulance. They telephoned a doctor, and the hospital. The hysterical girl on the sidewalk, and several neighbors who had witnessed the accident from afar, began to piece the story together. Telegraph wires grew hot with messages. Patrol wagons and motorcycles started on a chase for the automobile that had done the deed.

But Stephen Gardley lay white and still upon the bed in the dim hospital room with two doctors and several nurses hovering over him, a white, anguished mother kneeling by his side. And Philip Gardley, the boyish smile dead upon his stark set face, stood at the foot of the bed gripping the iron railing of the footboard, and watched his brother slowly dying in his stead.

For hours they waited there. It seemed like ages to the brother who had never in his life before had anything hard to bear. Minute by minute, hour after hour, Philip had to go over that scene, always beginning with that picture of his splendid, dependable brother standing there waiting for him with that smile of perfect contentment upon his lips.

He had to reconstruct everything that must have happened, to know all that had passed in his brother's mind in that one swift instant of comprehension and choice. It had to be one or the other of them, and Stephen had chosen to be the victim. There was not time to save them both! It was like Stephen to do it, of course. But considering all things, Philip recognized how much better it would have been for everyone if he had been the victim. Not better for himself! He shivered as he thought of himself lying there in pain with life slowly ebbing away. He had no conception of any such possibility for himself. Yet Stephen had unhesitatingly chosen death for himself, that he, Philip, irresponsible, selfish, might go on living. And he wasn't worth it! He knew in his heart that practically everyone, even his mother, would think so. Yet he had been left here to live, at such a cost, and Stephen had been struck down!

The awfulness of it all would roll over him overwhelmingly, till he longed to drop out of sight, out of existence, to call on the rocks and the mountains to hide him from the world that had so loved Stephen.

There was no phase of the terrible occurrence that did not force itself upon him as he stood there, on trembling limbs that threatened to crumple under him, gripping that white iron bar with hands that felt weak as water. It seemed that he grew ages older while he stood there watching that white face, swathed in bloodmarked bandages, those closed eyes, watching his mother's anguish, his own heart wrenched with the imminence of dreadful loss. How was he going to live without his brother?

All his life this brother had been safeguarding him, supplying him with what he needed, even fulfilling his every fancy, and how carelessly he had accepted it all! How as a matter of course he had taken it as only his due, and asked for more. Yes, and got it too! The expensive car, for instance! He had found afterward that the business was in straits just then and Stephen had had to drive a cheap secondhand car to manage the extra expense for him. And then his trip to Europe! And the partnership! Oh, the stabbing pain that shot through him at that thought! What would the business be with Stephen gone?

Oh, wasn't there something that could be done to save him even now?

Yet when he wildly sought the doctor in the hall and besieged him with questions, he only gravely shook his head, and sent him, desperate, back to grip that iron rail and watch for a possible flutter of those white eyelids. Oh, would there not be at least a word, a look, before he went from them forever?

And then, at last, it came—a look fully conscious, a slow smile of precious understanding and farewell that Philip would carry with him into eternity; a voice, low, vibrant, clear—Stephen's last words:

"It's all right, Phil. You'll carry on!"

A fleeting look of deep love into his mother's eyes, and he was gone!

Stephen was gone!

And he, Philip, was left to carry on!

How that thought came down upon his light and easy soul with crushing meaning! How the boy of a day ago shrank into himself and cried out in protest to a God he did not know. How he went through the interminable days of anguish that dragged themselves so unmercifully slowly until the funeral was over! His white, anguished face looked out as from the gloom of the valley of the shadow. People said, "How he loved him!" in slow astonished voices, and looked after him wonderingly. No one had thought that he had it in him to love and appreciate his brother so deeply.

But Philip did not hear them, did not see the surprise in their faces. He went the necessary way through those awful days up to the afternoon of the service in a kind of daze, seeing but one thought ever before him. He, Philip, would have been a dead man, if Stephen had not died for him! There had been no other possibility! Stephen had chosen to lay his splendid, successful life down in his place! Stephen had died that he might live, and therefore it was his place henceforth to die to himself that he might live Stephen's life for him. Stephen was an infinitely better man than Philip knew he ever could be, and now that Stephen was gone and the world could not see him nor know him anymore, it was his place to carry on Stephen's life as he had begun it, and it seemed an appalling thing that he was asked to do.

The day of the service, Philip sat by his mother, where she had chosen to stay, close by the casket where lay that sweet, strong face.

When Philip lifted his grief-filled eyes, there across the room sat Enid Ainsley, the pretty girl to whom he had been speaking when the accident occurred. He remembered how she had called some nothing across that had made him step nearer to hear her. Perhaps there had been a bit of self-consciousness on his own part as he moved toward her, because he knew that Stephen and his mother did not approve of his friendship with Enid. Yes, he knew that there was a fascination about her. He had owned to himself more than once that he was in love with her; yet now in the revulsion that this catastrophe had brought, she seemed almost an offense sitting there in her becoming costume of deep black. He could not bear to look at her. She seemed the cause of his great loss. He wished she had not come. Why should she weep in that hysterical way? It seemed to him that good taste should have kept her away.

Ah! She was one of the things that must be cut out of his life from henceforth. Stephen would never have hung around with a girl like Enid.

Yet even as he turned his eyes from looking at the girl, it came to him that Stephen would never have felt resentment toward her. He was always full of kindliness even toward those who had injured him.

And of course it was not Enid's fault that he had been standing there in the middle of the road talking to her when the peril came.

He groaned in spirit as the interminable service dragged along. He heard nothing of the comfort it was meant to give. He was thinking of his own lost life, thinking how he must now fit himself into his brother's place and live his life instead of his own.

He had no impatience toward this idea, no question but that of course he would do it. There was no question as to whether he would shirk this most uncongenial task. It was something that his inner nature demanded of him. It was just that his own bright, thoughtless life was dead, ended as thoroughly as if he had been crushed beside his brother there on the street by the murderous car; and he had entered into the life of another to live it out.

There might be a time when he could look back and be glad of the splendid foundation which his brother had laid for him to build upon, the best start possible that a young man could have in life. At present he could only be aghast.

He looked at the beautiful dead face in the coffin with a stern mask upon his own, struggling to keep his inner feelings from being seen by the world, for it seemed he was really looking upon his own face lying there among the flowers. He, Philip Gardley, dead with his brother! He knew he could never be his brother, much as he should try, and yet he must try, and equally he could not be himself because of trying.

The first night after the funeral was agony. Stephen's room empty! He could just remember how when he was a little boy Stephen was away at college for four long years. He seemed a great stranger-hero when he came back. But now it had been so very long that Stephen had been at home. Grammar school days and high school days and then college for himself, and always that wonderful older brother at home making things go, as his father would have done if he had lived. Why, it hadn't occurred to him that Stephen could ever die, at least not till he himself was an old, old man. Old man! Ah! He drew in his breath sharply. Would he have to live out that long, long life for Stephen? "Carry on!" Those were his last words! It seemed so interminable to Philip, lying in his bed, with Stephen's room closed, empty. No Stephen in the house, ever, anymore. He was to be Stephen now! Incredible thought!

He knew his mother was feeling the emptiness of the house, the agony of loss, too. Her door across the hall stood open. He could hear a soft sob now and then, quickly suppressed.

Stephen would have gone to comfort her if he had been here. He had always been like that. He could dimly remember Stephen comforting his mother when he was a tiny child; it must have been after his father's death, although he could not remember that.

Well, if he was to carry on, it was his place now to comfort his mother. Could he do it? He shrank from it inexpressibly. He doubted if he could. She had always comforted him—when Stephen wasn't there to do it. But now he was in Stephen's place and must not let her see how much he needed comfort himself. How old he felt!

He lay there trying to get the consent of himself to go and try to do what Stephen would have done; trying to imagine how one should go about comforting a mother; trying to fall asleep before he had actually decided if he must. But by and by his conscience, or something that answered for conscience in his hitherto carefree soul, prodded him beyond the limits and he stumbled up and across the hall, entering his mother's room almost stealthily, as if he might change his mind after all.

She had ceased sobbing. Perhaps she was asleep and it was not necessary. He could see the outline of her head on the pillow; her frail arm beneath the lacy sleeve was lifted, holding a handkerchief to her eyes. Then she gave a soft convulsive breath as of a suppressed moan, and his conscience drove him across the floor, while his soul was suggesting that his mother would probably think it odd of him to come.

She looked up as he approached the bed, half startled. The thought menaced him that perhaps she would not want him. Perhaps she even looked upon him as the cause of her beloved elder son's death, just as he had thought of that girl. Perhaps his mother shrank from him, and could not love him as she had. The thought went like a sword through his newly awakened soul, and twisted about painfully. He was standing over her now. Perhaps he should not have come. He felt abject. Should he go back? But he could not do that without saying something.

He dropped upon his knee beside the bed, bent over her, and felt his own tears start like a child. He wanted to hide his face in her neck and weep, tell her he could not carry on, ask her to comfort him as she had always done.

But he was a man! He could not do that! He was to *carry on!*

Blindly he groped with his lips and touched her eyelids, wet with tears, and then was stung with the thought that Stephen had always kissed her so, on her eyelids, and now he was taking Stephen's place. Oh, he ought not to have done that! Perhaps it would hurt her! What an everlasting blunderer he was! He could never learn to take Stephen's place without hurting. He couldn't be Stephen no matter how he tried! Stephen would not have done a tactless thing like that. He should have kissed her forehead as he had always done, lightly, or her lips. But no, he had to kiss her eyelids, the very thing that would remind her most of her loss! He wanted to turn and run away to hide in dismay at himself.

But the mother's arm suddenly went around him gently, and she reached her lips to his and murmured: "Philip! Dear son!" and Philip stole away again awkwardly, embarrassedly. He had done his best, and perhaps she liked it. She seemed to him as usual, yet somehow he knew he had not comforted her, only showed her that he was sorry and that he needed comfort himself. Stephen would have had words about heaven and hereafter. Stephen was that way. Philip groped around in his mind for some form of family tradition called religion that would help now, but nothing came to mind. Heaven seemed very far away and undesirable. One had to go on living and being somebody else. All the brightness of life was gone. He had to carry on for someone else.

He went down to the office in the morning with a heavy heart and a stern face. He called his brother's helpers about him and tried to gather up the threads that had been dropped by the head of the establishment, but though he conscientiously sought to understand, and asked many questions most earnestly, his mind seemed a blank. There was something hard and artificial about all that he did. He found himself trying to look older than he was, to appear as Stephen would have appeared.

"He's doin' the best he can," said the old Scotsman who had looked after the building since Stephen was first in business. "He's tryin' hard, but a body can't take the place o' thot mon. *Nae* body can!"

And, although the Scotsman did not know it, Philip heard him, gave him one keen glance, and went back to his office to drop his head upon his desk and groan in spirit. How could he carry on for Stephen? What could he do? What was lacking?

Day after day went by and his heart grew heavier. How could he keep it up? He went gravely from house to office and back again, going through the duties of each day carefully, precisely, becoming more proficient in their technique each day, yet getting no nearer to his goal. When strangers from out of town came in to do business they sought out the old helpers instead of the new head. They were missing Stephen and he could do nothing about it. He was making a miserable failure of it all! He was not taking Stephen's place even to his mother. He knew it. He was just Philip, the younger son, and she was grieving alone for Stephen, her dependence!

His mother roused to alarm at last, urged him to go out among his young friends, invite them home, bring some brightness about the house. But he shook his head.

"No, Mother, I couldn't. I'm done with all that!" he answered gravely to her pleading.

The circle of his friends talked him over.

"He might as well have died," said a young girl bitterly. "He's just like one dead. Or like a stranger! He looks at you from so far away! Whoever would have thought his brother's death would have made him like this? He can't bring Stephen back by acting like the tomb!"

And one day he heard two elderly men conversing. They did not know their voices carried to the seat behind them in the suburban train.

"Yes, he's settled down more than I ever dreamed he could," said one, a noted lawyer, whom he knew as a dear friend of his dead father. "I'm sure he's going to make a good man. He used to be a bit wild, but he seems to have given all that up. But he'll never be half the man his brother Stephen was!"

"Oh, no!" said the other who was a wealthy businessman and also an officer in the church he and his mother attended. "He lacks something. I wouldn't exactly say pep! He's taken hold of his business with a stern rigidity I wouldn't have expected of one so unstable as he was, but he lacks that deep vital spark that Stephen had, that was almost spirituality, even in business matters."

"Yes," said the lawyer thoughtfully, "Stephen was the most godlike man I ever knew. For so young a man it was most remarkable. It was almost as if Christ were come down and living his life for him. He fairly radiated God in his whole contact with the world."

Philip sat listening behind his sheltering newspaper and let the thought drive deep into his heart.

It carried real conviction with it. That was the matter with him. He was not godlike. Stephen had been godlike and he never could be. He was sure of that! It wasn't in him. Yet somehow, if he knew how to go about it, he would like to try.

When a mere boy in his teens he had joined the church. In a general way he had known himself for a sinner and admitted belief in the atoning sacrifice of the Savior. It seemed a kind benevolent thing for the Savior to have done to die on the cross in a general atonement, and he always felt that if there was some mistake about it and it should prove not to be true, it was at least "a peach of a fake," and a pleasant way to get through life to have a safe feeling about the hereafter. But he had scarcely given two thoughts to the matter since he united with the church. He felt that he had done all that was necessary. There remained but to live a fairly decent life and he would be eligible for any crowns that were to be handed out. Now, however, as he thought of Stephen and of what these two respected men had been saying, he saw that there must be something more. Stephen had been godlike. Well, then *he* would be godlike too! He would get to work and get for himself some real righteousness such as Stephen had.

To that end he suggested to his mother that they go to prayer meeting that night. Much surprised, she assented and they went, but he got very little help from that save a mild kind of self-satisfaction that he had gone. An old deacon took the service and droned out worn platitudes that did not reach beyond the surface.

But there was mention of a new leader for the Boy Scouts, as the old leader had resigned, and volunteers were called for. Philip thought it over and offered his own services. Perhaps this was the way to become godlike, to make himself what Stephen had been and make his life count for the things that had meant so much to Stephen.

They told him that a Sunday school class of boys went with the Scout organization, and after a moment's hesitation he took that over too. This was what Stephen would have been likely to do.

He wondered what he should teach those boys. He prepared some platitudes and realized hopelessly the boys' restlessness. The empty words he was giving them meant nothing, had no aim. They were letting them roll off their well-armored young souls like a shower of harmless shot. He wasn't getting anywhere. They didn't even like him very well. He could see that.

For weeks he went on dragging himself through duties, financial and spiritual, getting nowhere. Each week when a meeting was over he resolved to resign before the next, yet went on for Stephen's sake.

Someone asked him to address the Sunday school on Boys' Day because Stephen had always had such a wonderful message for the boys. He tried to do it, but saw through their politeness how bored they were. He had nothing to give them but more platitudes that they already knew by heart. He was really giving them some of the same old dry phrases he had hated so in speakers when he was a boy.

That night he got down upon his knees and wept in the dark. He actually spoke to God and told him he was a failure; that he couldn't go on any longer; that God, if there was a God who expected him to carry on, must help! He couldn't do another thing alone!

And then, almost as an answer, there came the idea of going to the minister for help. The minister had never struck him as being a man to whom one could easily go in trouble. He was a conservative, elderly, rather formal man; but a minister *ought* to be able to help in a case like this, oughtn't he? He was supposed to help the soul to God, wasn't he? And Stephen had always respected him.

So, late at night, almost midnight it was, he took his hat and went out, walking down the street on what to him seemed a very hopeless errand. But it was a last resort.

A stranger opened the door, a younger man than the minister, a man with disarming eyes and a burr on his tongue that came from across the water. Philip liked him. His eyes had something in them that reminded him of Stephen.

The stranger explained that the minister had gone out to see a dying man and he was waiting up for him. He said the minister might be back soon, and opened the door with such a friendly warmth that Philip stepped in, wondering at himself for doing it.

He was not in a mood for talking with strangers, and the minister would not want to be kept up any longer after he got home. He should have waited until another time. When he was inside he said so, intending to go home at once. But the stranger, who said his name was McKnight, looked at him with that disarming smile and said:

"Is there anything that I could do for you? I am a servant of the Lord Jesus also, and shall be glad if there is any way that I can help you."

Philip never knew how it came about. Certainly he had no intention of taking that stranger into his confidence. But he found himself sitting in the cozy library telling this man with the holy eyes just what was happening in his life and how unhappy he was.

Just a few questions and the kindly stranger, who had amazingly become a friend, had the whole story of Philip's life.

"And so, my friend," said the stranger, "your brother was a man who knew the Lord Jesus, and had the power of the resurrection in his life. And you are trying to be your brother without knowing his Lord or having the right to that power! Is that it?"

"I don't know what you mean by the resurrection power," said Philip.

"The resurrection power is the life Christ brought from the tomb when he rose from the dead," answered McKnight. "It is his life that came out of death—'the life whereby Jesus conquered death.' If you have that power within you, it will enable you to live a life on a higher plane than ordinary living. You want to be godlike? There is no other power that can make you show forth the God-Man Christ Jesus but the power of his resurrection."

"That's all Greek to me," said Philip with bewildered eyes. "I never learned the language you are speaking."

"Well, I'll put it more simply," said the stranger. "You can't be like a man unless you know him, can you?"

"You can't even if you do know him," said Philip sadly. "I've known my brother all my life, and I've tried my best to be like him, and let his life go on in me, and I find it can't be done."

"But are you quite sure that you knew him?" asked the keen-eyed questioner. "You have found something about him into which you cannot enter, his godlikeness that people speak of. Did you ever know your brother in this phase of his experience? Did you ever get to know thoroughly his inmost heart on this matter?"

Philip stared, then answered quickly: "No, I wouldn't let him talk to me about religious matters. I wasn't interested."

"Exactly. Then how could you know him thoroughly, and how could you be like him in that respect if you never went with him through his deepest experiences?"

"I suppose I couldn't," said Philip hopelessly. "Then you think there's no use?"

"No! Oh no! I think there is great use. It is quite true that your *brother's* life can never go on in you, but you *can* know his Christ, who made your brother godlike. The Lord Jesus Christ is willing to live his resurrection life through you, if you will, as much as he ever did through your brother. That is a miracle, of course, but we are speaking of heavenly things, you see."

"How could one know Christ?" Philip's tone was full of awe.

"The first step is to accept him as your own personal Savior. When you do that his Spirit takes up his dwelling in you. Then surrender to him so utterly that you actually reckon your self-life to have died with him on the cross, so that you can say: 'I am crucified with Christ: nevertheless I live; yet not I, but Christ liveth in me: and the life which I now live in the flesh I live by the faith of the Son of God, who loved me, and gave himself for me.' Isn't that substantially the same thing that you have been trying to do for your brother, to die to your own life so that the life of your brother might go on in the same channels it had when he was living?"

"It is," said Philip with dawning comprehension.

"Well, that's all, only put Christ in your brother's place. It is *Christ* whose life must go on through yours; for I am sure that is what happened in your brother's life. It was Christ who was living in him, not Stephen Gardley. And when his body was crushed it was Christ whose resurrection power was hindered, through having one less human life to dwell in. Did it ever occur to you that the Lord Jesus can be seen today only through men and women who are willing to have self slain with all its old programs, standards, ambitions, desires, aims, will, and let Christ take up his abode in them? The world saw Jesus through your brother because your brother counted himself as crucified with him, and was therefore under that promise in Romans 6: 'For if we have been planted together in the likeness of his death, we shall be also in the likeness of his resurrection.... Likewise reckon ye also yourselves to be dead indeed unto sin but alive unto God through Jesus Christ our Lord.' You see, my friend, the death and resurrection of Christ is the power of God, and you have a right to it in your life if you are willing for this death-union with Christ himself.

"But it is not to be acquired by any effort of your own. It is only through the death of self that he can come in. There is not room for him and you both, and the natural man must go because God can do nothing with him. The old sinful nature cannot inherit the kingdom of heaven."

Philip listened in wonder as the way was made plain. He was deeply moved at the stranger's prayer for him, and finally went home to read his Bible.

McKnight had sent him to the story of the crucifixion, and straight through the four Gospels he read it, till the scene was printed as vividly on his mind as the death of his own brother. For the first time since Stephen's death, Philip lost sight of that bloodstained face lying in the dust of the road, and saw his Savior hanging on the cross instead. He felt the shame, the scoffs, the insults, quivered at the nails driven in the tender hands and feet, saw the trickling blood from the thorn-crown, the awful spear thrust!

Ah! This was the one who had died that he might live *eternally!* And this King of all the earth wanted to live out his life through him! He was asked to "carry on" for the Savior of the world!

It was just before daybreak that he turned out his light and knelt beside his open window with the morning star still shining, the dawn creeping softly into the sky, and surrendered to his risen Lord; confessed all his own unworthiness, his vain efforts of the flesh to be like another *man;* laid down himself to die with his Lord and said: "I am crucified with thee, Lord Jesus. Nevertheless I live, yet not I, Philip Gardley, but Christ liveth *in* me, and the life which I now live in the flesh I live by the faith of the Son of God, who loved me, and gave himself for me!"

Then a new day began.

He went downstairs to breakfast with a different look in his face. He bent over his anxious mother tenderly and kissed her. He said:

"Mother, I've found the Lord Jesus, and it's going to be all different now!"

They began to feel it almost at once in the office, and as the days went by.

"That young man is growing like his brother!" one of the office force said.

"He is growing like Jesus Christ!" said an old friend of his father's who happened to be in the office at the time.

"Well, I suppose you're right," said the first. "That was really what I meant, I guess!" and his voice had a note of awe in it.

But then because the enemy never lets a chance go by to hinder a newborn soul, Enid Ainsley came into his life again.

Someone had asked her into the church choir for a special musical festival, for she had a really marvelous voice and was besides quite decorative, with her gold hair, her vivid complexion, and her great blue eyes. Philip also had promised to help with the music and Enid managed it quite easily that he should take her home from the rehearsals.

At first he treated her gravely, pleading business and hurrying away at once. but soon she inveigled him into her home and tried to bring back the old free and easy camaraderie.

She played her part cleverly, leading him on to almost hope that perhaps she too was changing.

One night he tried to tell her of his own experience and the new hope that had come into his life. But she flung away from him.

"Oh, for pity's sake, Phil, aren't you ever going to be yourself again?" she cried out impatiently.

"I hope not," he said gravely.

"Well, I think it's silly, this trying to be like your brother! It was well enough to respect his memory for awhile and all that, but it gets boring to keep it up. For heaven's sake, snap out of it, and quickly, too."

"I'm not trying to be like my brother any longer," he said quietly. "I found it was impossible, because, you know, it wasn't he who was living in him, it was another."

"What do you mean?"

"I mean the Lord Jesus Christ."

"For heaven's sake!" she turned upon him. "Are you turning religious? Phil Gardley gone religious! Well, that's a great joke. That's *precious!* I'll have to tell the gang."

"No," said Philip steadily. "Philip Gardley hasn't gone religious. Philip Gardley has died! Christ who died for me is living his life in me. Henceforth it's not to be my life, but his. Enid, this thing is very real to me. It's not a joke. And Enid, I want you to let me tell you about it. I want you to know him too. Enid, I've been loving you for a long time—"

Then Enid used all her guiles to turn his attention to herself and his love for her.

But Philip gently brought back the subject again and again, urging her to accept his Lord also, until at last she flouted out upon him with a cold hard look on her lovely face.

"I'm tired of this," she said haughtily. "I don't care to share your love with anyone else, even *God!* You can choose between us. Either you give up this fanatical nonsense or I'm done with you once and for all."

He pleaded with her. He tried to make her understand that the thing had been *done*. That he was no longer in a position to choose. He had died with Christ on that cross long ago! He had given his word! But she only turned from him coldly; and at last he went away, sadly, with a break in his heart.

At home he knelt before his Lord and struggled

long. Was earthly love to be denied him? Why could not this beautiful woman be drawn by God's Spirit to love his Lord?

It was a long hard struggle, his will against God's will. But was that dying with Christ? He was startled at the thought.

Worn with the struggle, he flung himself upon his bed, and sharply the words of the young Scotsman came back to him:

"It is just in the measure that the 'I' has been crucified in your life, that Christ in the power of his resurrection can be revealed to the world through you."

Torn between his desire to have his own way, and his growing realization of what it might mean to his Christian witness if he married this girl, he dropped finally into an uneasy sleep. His last thought was a prayer that God would somehow make Enid what she ought to be, and give her to him.

And then there came to him a vision of Christ, standing there at the foot of his bed, with the print of the nails in his hands, and the thorns upon his brow, looking deep into Philip Gardley's soul.

"You and I died on Calvary together, Philip," he said. "Are you remembering that? And now, if I give you what you are asking for, this girl will come between you and me! Are you prepared for that? Are you *willing* for that? She belongs to the world and cares only for the things of the world. She will not accept me as her Savior! You will have to choose between us as she has said. You may have your way if you will, but you must understand that it will lead you through distress and sorrow, and although I shall never cease to love you, it will separate you and me in our walk together. It will also prevent you from showing my resurrection power to the world. The world will not be able to see me through you if you choose this way. Can you not trust me that this is not best for you?"

He awoke startled, and the struggle went on, but at last he yielded, kneeling low before his Lord and crying out:

At thy feet I fall,
Yield thee up my all,
To suffer, live or die,
For my Lord crucified.

Out into the world he went, a different world, where a closed door had utterly changed his course. And one day he found a bit of a poem in a magazine, lying on a desk in a room where he had to wait for an interview:

Is there some door closed by the Father's hand,
Which widely open you had hoped to see?
Trust God, and wait—for when he shuts the door
He keeps the key!

The days went by and strange things followed. Disaster suddenly surrounded him on every hand. The bank closed that held his financial situation in its grasp. The business went to the wall and he had to begin all over again. There were perils and perplexities everywhere. But still his Christian witness grew brighter. People marveled at the way he took his testings. He was walking through it all in the daily consciousness of Christ as his constant companion. He was able to say as the days went by, each bringing its new problem:

I do not ask my cross to understand,
*   My way to see;*
Better in darkness just to feel thy hand
*   And follow thee.*

There came a Sunday when he sat in a shadowed seat back under the gallery of the Sunday school room during the review of the Sunday school lesson by the superintendent. Suddenly the superintendent asked a question.

"Children, did any of you ever see anybody who made you think of Jesus Christ? Who seemed like what you would expect of Jesus Christ if he were to come back here in visible form?"

A quick eager hand went up, Jimmy Belden, one of Philip's Boy Scouts.

"Well, Jimmy?" said the superintendent.

Jimmy stood up promptly and in a clear voice said, "Mr. Philip Gardley!"

Then did Philip Gardley bow his head and cover his eyes with his hand, his heart filled with glad humility. God had given him that great honor and privilege of being able to show Christ in some small measure at least, to that one Boy Scout, and perhaps to give him some little idea of what that life was whereby Jesus conquered death! It thrilled him with a joy inexpressible and brought tears of humility to his eyes.

And that night as he stood by his window looking up to the stars and thought of it all, his heart recalled a verse he had read that day:

He was better to me than all my hopes,
Better than all my fears,
He made a bridge of my broken works,
And a rainbow of my tears.
The billows that guarded my sea-girt path
But bore my Lord on their crest!
When I dwell on the days of my wilderness march
I can lean on his love and rest!

THE MINISTER'S SON

FAITH Holden arrived at her sister Myra's home about the middle of the afternoon, after a three years' stay abroad. She was welcomed joyously by the entire family, including her minister brother-in-law, and the seven children, of whom Joy, aged ten, was the youngest, and Barry, aged nineteen, the oldest. In between there were Rosalie, John, the twins Jean and Joan, and Steve.

They welcomed their guest so eagerly that it was some minutes before they realized that they had not yet taken her into the house. Then they roused to their duties and escorted her upstairs to the guest room, and one by one drifted away to their various interests, leaving the two sisters alone for a good long talk, the kind of talk that people who love one another, and have been separated for a long time, do enjoy so much.

Faith settled down in the big winged chair by the

window, where she could watch the changes that had come in her sister's plump, contented face.

"And now tell me all about everything!" she said. "It's easy to see you are well and happy." She laughed.

Then followed the details of all that had only been touched upon in letters, details that made the past live again.

At last the elder sister rose.

"I'm talking you to death and you ought to rest, Faith. For, you know, I have a plan for this evening. I'm hoping you'll feel you can go to a meeting with us tonight! We're having such a wonderful evangelist. He's been with us in the church for three weeks and this is his last week. I was so glad when I found you would get here before he leaves. He has taken the town by storm. They even close the shops for an hour in the afternoon because everybody wants to go to the afternoon meeting. Do you think you'll be too tired to go?"

"Why, of course not, Myra. I'll be as eager to hear him as you are to have me. And the children? Do they all go out to the meeting? Nobody has to stay at home with them? As I remember it they were all Christians when I left, except the two youngest. Have they come into the fold?"

"Oh, yes, they're all church members. Our little Joy united at the last communion, and she's very much interested in her Sunday school class, and the catechism class and all. She and Steve have been quite prominent in the children's meetings we've been having in connection with the evangelistic campaign. They go out after school and distribute Gospels and tracts and invitations, and they've brought all their school friends to the meetings. No, nobody has to stay at home with them. They are all deeply interested and working in the meetings. That is, all except Barry."

The mother sighed and looked troubled.

"Except *Barry?*" said the aunt. "Why, I thought I remembered Barry as being a very remarkable young Christian when he was just a little fellow!"

"Yes, he was," said the mother, knitting her brows and giving another sigh, "but somehow he's got switched off the track. No, it's not college. He goes to a strictly fundamental college, and he's well taught. I don't think he has any doubts at all about the great truths of Christianity. He never has expressed any. He just isn't interested, that's all, and when you try to talk to him about it he looks at you in a strange way and says what you're saying is a lot of 'hooey.' It's the strangest thing! Once I pressed him hard to tell me what was the matter, and his answer was, 'Well I can't see it, that's all. Nobody is sincere! It's all a lot of baloney!' "

"Sincere?" said his aunt, startled. "With such a wonderful father and mother!"

"That's it!" said his mother earnestly. "Not that I'm anything, but he has such a wonderful father. He surely must see that! Of course his father says this is just a phase, and he'll outgrow it. I'm sure I hope he will. It's terribly distressing. You see, he doesn't go to church anymore, and that's *so* mortifying when his father is the minister!"

"Doesn't go to church?" said Aunt Faith, aghast.

"No," said Barry's mother, "I don't believe he's been inside the church for more than a year. We've coaxed and done everything we know how to do. We've even tried to bribe him to go again, but it doesn't do a bit of good. He just shuts his lips tight and something hard glints in his eyes, and he says, '*No.*' His father even offered to make a good big down-payment on a new car for him if he would go to church for a year, but he said no, he'd get his own car! And he *did!* I am sure I don't know where he goes instead of church, but he's never there anymore."

There were tears in her eyes as she looked up sorrowfully.

"Then he hasn't heard this wonderful evangelist speak at all!"

"No, he hasn't heard him! The night we had him here to dinner hoping he'd get acquainted with Barry, Barry didn't come home at all until way after midnight!"

"Oh!" said Aunt Faith softly, pitifully. "That's so sad. I can't realize that is possible. I'm sure Barry was saved when he was a child! How he used to love to hear the Bible stories, and how earnestly he prayed! Oh, I'm sure he was saved. And when once a soul is saved, God never lets go of his own, you know. We'll have to get together regularly every day, you and I, and make it a special subject of prayer. He's a child of the faith! He'll come back. We'll *pray*. Of course you and John have been praying, I know, but we'll pray together. We'll take that verse, '. . . if two of you shall agree on earth as touching anything that they shall ask, it shall be done for them. . . .' I have great faith in that promise."

Barry's mother gave her sister a startled look.

"I've prayed, yes, but I really haven't had much faith lately. I'm afraid Barry's just grown up and got away from God. Of course his father is quite sure we needn't worry. He says Barry will come back into church work someday. But I don't know, I'm sure!" and she sighed again.

"When did he begin to get this way?" asked the aunt thoughtfully. "What was the cause?"

"I'm sure I don't know. He just began criticizing Christians, that was all. We reprimanded him, of course, but he only laughed. He said it was all bunk what they said, that they didn't live up to what they preached. As nearly as I can remember he came in one day and told his father that the senior elder was a liar. He said he told one man something and then told another the exact opposite. His father told him that of course he just didn't understand, and he must never talk that way about a good man again. 'Good man, my eye!' said Barry, 'If he's a good man, lead me from him. He's a *liar!*' And then a few days later he came and told me the president of the women's missionary society was an old hypocrite. I said, 'Oh, Barry! Remember what your father said!' And he said, 'You just ought to hear her talk to her milkman! You'd see what I mean.' There! There he comes now. Don't let him know we've been talking about him!"

And then they could hear Barry come whistling up the stairs. He came and stood in his aunt's doorway, leaning against the door frame, beaming.

"Oh, say! Aunt Faith, it's good to have you back again!" he said. "I've missed you a lot. You and I used to be great pals, didn't we?"

"We did." His aunt laughed tenderly. "And you don't know how I missed you. Do you know, Barry, I always felt that you prolonged my youth ten years at least. You were as good company as a grown person."

"Well," said Barry earnestly. "I'll say you were a wonderful friend for a kid to have! I'll never forget all you did for me. All those picture puzzles you got for me, real grown-up ones, and taught me how to put them together, watching colors and forms! And then all those stone blocks you bought, six whole boxes! And helped me to build bridges and railroad stations and towers and churches and bungalows. I'm in an architect's office this summer, and doing real well, they tell me, and I believe it was you who gave me my bent for architecture. Do you know, I've got all those blocks yet, and I love every one of them, especially those little blue slates for the roof. Got them locked in my closet. Of course I did let the kids play with them for a while till I found Joy biting her teeth through on some of them; she had taken little nicks out of their nice sharp edges. And then one day

I found Steve had built a castle out of them in his goldfish bowl, and the water was disintegrating them, so I took 'em away. I had to send to the manufacturer to replace some of them, but I've got them all now, every one, put away in the box according to the picture on the cover. And by the way, that was the cleverest way to make a kid pick up his toys! Why, I loved to put 'em away in the box according to the picture, as well as I did to get them out to build. Say, I'd like to build a bungalow now!"

"Why, so would I, Barry," said Aunt Faith with a twinkle of appreciation. "Let's do it while I'm here!"

"All right, that's a bargain!" said Barry. "How about tomorrow afternoon? I'll get home early from the office and we can work awhile before dinner. You never can do anything in the evenings in this house anymore. *Every*body goes to church!" He laughed almost bitterly.

Suddenly his mother spoke up: "And by the way, Barry, I wonder if you wouldn't like to take Aunt Faith over to the meeting tonight? She wants to go, and I have to run around to see Mrs. Parsons after dinner. She fell downstairs last night and broke her leg and she's sent for me. She wants me to take a notice for the Ladies' Aid to be given out in the meeting tonight. Rosalie and the twins have to go to the hotel to bring some girls to the meeting; and you can't depend on the rest, they have Junior Choir practice. I thought your aunt wouldn't want to go too early after her long journey. Will you take her?"

Barry looked up with a frown and a whimsical expression, as if his eyes were understanding more than his mother expected him to. He straightened up and looked at his mother. Was this another scheme to get him to go to church? And was Aunt Faith in it too? Then he looked quickly at his aunt.

But Aunt Faith looked up with a protest.

"No, Barry, don't you *think* of it!" she said quickly before he could answer his mother. "I haven't been away so long that I have forgotten the way to the church, and I'm not at all shy about going in alone. Don't change any of your plans for the evening on my account, please. I would feel most uncomfortable to have you do so."

And all the time behind Barry's back Barry's mother was signaling frantically with appealing eyes and shaking her head, but Aunt Faith finished her protest in spite of it.

"Barry, really, I mean it. I don't want one of you children to change any of your plans for me. I don't want to be a nuisance!"

Barry's face relaxed.

"Why, Aunt Faith, you *couldn't* be a nuisance!" he said. "Sure I'll take you to church if you want to go. Do you still like to sit in the gallery?"

"I adore it!" said Aunt Faith with a twinkle.

"All right, I'll get you the first seat in the synagogue. I suppose you want to see the whole show, don't you? Well, we'll go early. I'll take you down in my flivver."

Then with a smile he turned and strode past his astonished mother, down to the telephone in the lower hall. A moment later his mother, hurrying downstairs to look after some dinner arrangements, heard Barry at the telephone calling off a date with a girl!

She hustled right up the back stairs to her sister's room.

"Faith, you aren't asleep yet, are you? Isn't it *wonderful* that Barry's going to church! Now you'll be sure to get a good chance to work on him, won't you? Make him see how badly he's been treating us, how mortifying it is for the minister's son to stay away from church this way when the whole town is present."

"Oh, I wouldn't think that was nice, would you, Myra?" said Aunt Faith. "I'm sure he wouldn't care to come again if I began to lambast him about it the first thing. You just pray about it, Myra dear, and I will, and let us leave the rest to the Lord! The Holy Spirit knows how to bring conviction to his soul better than you and I do."

"Oh, but I think he ought to be made to see that he should go to church for *our* sakes, even if he isn't interested for his own, don't you?"

"Why, no," said the sister, "I don't know that I do. That wouldn't attain the real end for which you are anxious, would it? You want him to come because he desires to please the Lord, not *us*, don't you?"

"Oh, well, of course he would come to that," said the worried mother, "if he only would just get into things and hear what goes on. How can he expect to be interested if he doesn't hear anything? He needs to see how others are taking hold of this work. He needs to understand how popular this young preacher is."

"I'm not so sure," said Aunt Faith gravely. "Of course those influences do help in many instances, but it is something deeper than that we want, isn't it? We want him to come back to God, to get into communion with him, to go to church to worship him. I really don't believe just urging people to go to a meeting for your sake is going to help much. Nobody can come to God in the first place unless the Holy Spirit draws him. Nobody can come back to God when he has wandered away unless the Holy Spirit draws him. Only then can a soul really *want* God, you know."

"But don't you think Barry ought to come out of respect to his father?"

"Undoubtedly he ought, but that isn't the main thing. He ought to come out of respect to God. He ought to come to get near his Savior!"

"Oh, yes, of course," said Barry's mother anxiously. "But surely, Faith, you believe in inviting people to meetings?"

"Why, of course," said Aunt Faith, "*invite*, but not insist, not nag. Barry seems to be going of his own free will tonight. It may be only because he wants to be polite to me. But I should think our part was to pray that the Holy Spirit may open his heart to receive what he hears, and that you and I and the rest of us Christians shall not hinder the work of the Holy Spirit by anything in us that is awry."

"*Hinder?*" said the mother. "How could we hinder

the work of the Holy Spirit in Barry's life?"

"Well, I wouldn't be expected to know, would I?" said Aunt Faith. "But let's pray that if there is anything in us that is hindering, that God will open our eyes to it, shall we?"

"Why, of course," said the minister's wife a little stiffly, as if she were promising something utterly unnecessary. "But, Faith, if you get a good *chance*, you *will* speak to Barry, won't you? You know I've been depending on you to bring Barry to his senses."

"Well," smiled Faith, "if I were you I'd stop depending on me and begin to depend entirely on the Holy Spirit."

"You dear old sermonizer!" exclaimed her sister, suddenly coming up and kissing her again. "You always did live in the clouds, didn't you? Now, you lie down and get a good nap before the dinner bell rings! We have to have dinner exactly at six, you know, because the children go to the young people's choir practice at quarter before seven, and it makes everything so hurried if we are not on time."

But Faith Holden did not lie down for a nap immediately. Instead she locked her door and knelt down by her bed to pray for Barry.

Dinner was a hurried affair. Everybody was anxious to be off. Each one felt that his business was the most important. They all wanted to be waited on first, and then each wanted a second helping before the father had quite got around the first time. Then they all clamored for their dessert. But at last they all hastened away to their various engagements, till only Barry and Aunt Faith were left.

Barry was embarrassed. He thought they weren't treating Aunt Faith very well this first night of her homecoming.

"They're all so terribly busy!" he said apologetically. "Even the kid thinks the whole universe rests on her shoulders." But Aunt Faith only smiled and gave Barry another piece of pie and another cup of coffee.

"Oh, Barry," she said, "it's great to be sitting here looking at you, and you almost a man. It seems just the other day that you were born. I remember the first time I ever saw you. You were just eight days old. The nurse brought you to me and said, 'Here! Take this young man and get him to sleep! I've got to go down in the kitchen and get his mother something to eat.' And you stared up at me as if you were saying: 'Hello! You're somebody new, aren't you?' And I said, 'Yes, I'm somebody new, and we're going to have a grand time together.' And you stared on as if you were saying, 'You're somebody, and I'm somebody all by myself.' And I said, 'Yes, and now let's go look at the pictures on the wall. That's your grandmother in that big gold frame up there. She's a good scout. She'll make gingerbread men with currant eyes for you. Um-m! You'll like her! And that's your grandfather in that next frame. He's a good scout too! He'll ride you on his foot. You'll like that! And there in the next frames are your great grandmother and your great grandfather. You'll like them. And here on this wall are your aunts and uncles. Oh you'll have a grand time with them! Uncle John, and Uncle Rand, and Uncle Sam, and Uncle

Will, and Aunt Emily and Aunt Mary and Aunt Sue and Aunt Carolyn. They're swell persons. And over on this wall are all your cousins, Emmy Lou and Betty and Jane and Lynne and Fred and Sam and Nicky. Oh what fun you'll have with them! Playing hide and go seek, and drop the handkerchief, and baseball; skating and sliding downhill. You'll have wonderful fun.' And you stared at me and never winked, as if you were taking it all in and enjoying it. Then I began to sing to you. I sang lullabies and old hymns. I remember I sang 'How firm a foundation, ye saints of the Lord, is laid for your faith in his excellent Word,' and a lot of other hymns, and you kept staring at me without winking. And I thought, 'Will this baby *never* go to sleep?' At last your lashes went slowly down on your cheeks. But then they flashed open again as if you were afraid you would miss something. After a little, though, they slowly went down again. Now and then they would lift a bit to see if I was still there. But at last your lashes rested on your cheeks, and I went cautiously over to the bed and laid you down, with your head on the pillow, slipping my hand carefully out from under your head, pulling up the little blue silk quilt, putting pillows about you so you wouldn't fall off, and you were asleep!"

Barry listened radiantly till she had finished and then he said, "Why, Aunt Faith. I almost remember that! If I would think a little harder I'm sure I could remember it clearly. Your face has always reminded me of something pleasant in my past, and it must have been that."

As they rose from the table Barry caught Aunt Faith's fingers and squeezed them lovingly.

"Oh, Aunt Faith, I'm so glad you're here!" he said genuinely. "You're so sincere, and you don't *fuss!*"

"Thank you," she said, pressing his fingers affectionately. "That makes me very proud to have you say that!"

They sat for awhile on the porch talking. Barry told her all about the changes on the street.

"See that old house over there on the corner? Do you remember the old ramshackle porch with the pillars all tottering? Well, one day they fell down, and the man had to build a new porch. See those stone arches? Well, I took my stone blocks over there and built porch with arches for him, and he got the idea and built it. Good work, isn't it? That was the first house I ever 'architected.'

"And see that new house next door to the corner? There's a new bride and groom living there. We don't know them yet, but I don't believe we want to. She's got her face all painted up, and she has plucked eyebrows; her lips are so red they look as if they were bleeding. She's a mess, if you ask me!

"And next door the woman ran away with another man and left her family. He lives at a club, and the children are in boarding schools. The house is closed. It's awful!

"And next door the Millers still live there just as they did. They're kind of drying up. They never go out anywhere.

"And over on this side the Burtons don't do a thing but play bridge and have wild parties. Sometimes you can hear them laugh half the night.

"The house next to them is sold. We don't know yet who bought it. Isn't it painted an awful color? Sort of like pea soup!

"And over here at the left the Parkers still survive, poor as ever and twice as proud! And next to them is Dilly Peterson's cottage. Remember her? Yes, she still lives there, and she's *just* as *disagreeable* as ever!"

He talked on about the other houses up the street, comments for all. Then presently he jumped up, looking at his watch.

"Well, I guess it's time we got started. Will it take you long to get ready?"

"Oh, no. I've just got to get my hat," said Aunt Faith.

So Barry brought his car around and they were soon spinning down the street.

As they drew near to the church Barry was surprised to see so many people going in. He thought he had started very early. And then he was surprised again to see who some of the people were who were entering the church.

"I wonder how they got that old bird!" he said, looking wonderingly at one middle-aged man who was going in. "I never heard he went to church anywhere! He's supposed to be an atheist!"

The church was beginning to fill up when they arrived. Barry led his aunt to the gallery and found a front seat overlooking the audience, not far from a big window where there was a delightful breeze. Down below the people were filing in quickly now, and Aunt Faith was interested in recognizing old acquaintances. Barry kept up a running commentary on them, giving résumés of their history to date, and occasionally amusing comments on their characteristics.

"Quite a mob!" he said, with a kind of sneering wonder in his eyes. It was plain from some of his cryptic sentences that he was amazed to see some of the people who were there. Occasionally he branded one in contempt with the name "hypocrite," but for the most part his remarks were pleasant enough.

Then the organ began to play and the choir filed in. The platform had been extended to accommodate an augmented choir, and in front of the choir seats were two rows of little chairs from the primary room for the children. After the regular choir was seated, from the front door came marching the children led by Joy and another little girl; they looked like sweet little saints in their white dresses and their gold curls. Then came the little boys marching behind. And as they marched they sang:

Wide, wide as the ocean,
   High as the heavens above,
Deep, deep as the deepest sea,
   Is my Savior's love;
And I, though all unworthy
   Still am a child of his care,
For his Word teaches me
   That his love reaches me
Ev'rywhere.

Aunt Faith did not seem to be watching Barry, but her heart was on the alert and she missed not one of the expressions that flitted over his face as he watched his little sister in her white dress, with her bright head lifted and her eager face lighted, marching with the other children down the aisle and filing up to the platform. They sat there looking like so many flowers. The whole incident made a very lovely setting for the meeting that followed.

The leader prayed and Aunt Faith's heart gave thanks. He sounded sincere. She hoped Barry thought so.

Aunt Faith noticed with delight how the singing began to swell and ring out until it almost seemed as if the roof were being lifted. Even Barry seemed to enjoy it, though he did not move his lips to join in it.

When the young evangelist came on the platform Barry studied him keenly, critically. Aunt Faith saw the suggestion of an open mind perhaps, in his glance, but a settled conviction in the set of Barry's lips that this man too was probably a pleasant kind of fake. Still he studied him. And oh, how his aunt prayed that the man who was about to lead the service and give the message might be filled with wisdom from on high!

There followed more singing, enthusiastic, eager, soul-stirring. They sang a number of choruses: "The blood, the blood, is all my plea, Hallelujah, it cleanseth me!" "Calvary covers it all, my past with its sin and shame," and then another which Aunt Faith had never heard before:

I have the love of Jesus, love of Jesus,
  Down in my heart,
Down in my heart, down in my heart,
  I have the love of Jesus, love of Jesus,
Down in my heart,
  Down in my heart to stay.

Barry looked down with an amused sneer on his handsome lips. Aunt Faith's soul shrank away from the sight. It was a sneer of disillusionment, such as an older person might have worn. He was too young to look like that over the enthusiastic singing of a hymn. What could have made him feel that way? Barry, brought up in such a wonderful Christian family!

The audience burst into another verse:

I have the peace that passeth understanding,
  Down in my heart,
Down in my heart, down in my heart,
  I have the peace that passeth understanding,
Down in my heart,
  Down in my heart to stay.

And then Barry snickered right out; almost a snort of mirth, it was. But no, there was more than mere mirth, there was scoffing! Oh, he smothered it quickly behind his hand, but Aunt Faith was startled. What could have happened to Barry to convulse him with mirth about a tender song like that? Did he see something funny in the audience? No, he didn't seem to be looking at anything in particular. Yet again there was that hard, unbelieving look in his eyes.

Barry, her dear boy, Barry!

Then there were prayers. Many prayers, all over the house, most of them brief, only a few sentences, but tender and from the heart.

But Barry didn't even bow his head or close his eyes. He folded his arms and leaned over the railing, identifying each voice as it came, sometimes looking amused, sometimes thoughtful, sometimes sneering again. He didn't even bow his head when his own gray-haired father closed the prayers with a tender petition.

Aunt Faith's heart grew heavy, and she began to pray again for Barry.

They sang one or two more songs and then there were testimonies. All over the house the young people rose and testified, sometimes two or three were standing at once, giving their witness in clear voices.

Barry and Aunt Faith looked down at them, and Aunt Faith's heart thrilled as the testimonies went on.

That was Rosalie down there standing now.

"I want to say that the Lord is dearer to me today than ever before. He is helping me to know what the 'peace that passeth understanding' means."

And Barry suddenly snorted right out.

Oh, he put his hand over his mouth, and tried to clear his throat and convey the idea that he had not laughed, but Aunt Faith, looking furtively at him, saw a fleeting grin on his lips. His pretty sister sat down and several other young people arose to testify. But somehow the aunt got the impression that Barry was not being helped by this part of the meeting, that he seemed to see something behind it all which she could not understand. She found herself wishing that the testimony meeting would be over, for it certainly was not getting across with Barry.

But the testimonies went on. John stood up.

"I am trusting in the blood of Jesus to cover my sins!" he said with a manly ring to his voice, and his brother watching, grinned again. That clear testimony hadn't meant a thing to Barry! Why?

A moment later the twins arose: "I am glad that I have found peace in Jesus," said Jean.

Barry snickered faintly.

"Jesus is all the world to me. I think he is giving me victory over my sins!" said Joan.

Again Barry had difficulty in controlling his laughter, his hard unloving laughter and scorn.

Then over on the other side, away up front, Steve stood up and piped in his clear, boyish treble: "I am not ashamed of the gospel of Christ. For it is the power of God unto salvation!"

Barry frowned and drew a deep, disapproving sigh.

A little later Joy stood up in the front row of the children's choir and said in a soft, sweet voice, "I'm glad Jesus died for me. 'We love him because he first loved us.' "

It was very moving. Aunt Faith found the tears coming into her eyes, but turning suddenly she saw only an annoyed look on the face of the young man beside her. It was as if he were wishing that his family wouldn't say these things. His lips were shut again in that thin line of disapproval. There was no light of either wonder or awe in his eyes.

After that he sat back with his arms folded, and that inscrutable look on his young face. A look that showed as plainly as words could have done that as far as Barry was concerned, the meeting was ended. He had no further interest in what would follow. And in spite of her great desire, and her hope that had grown out of her own prayers, she had a sinking feeling, a certain conviction that nothing now would get across into this young man's heart.

And what was the secret of it? Why should the lovely testimonies of his own dear brothers and sisters, and even the clear ringing testimony of his mother, which came a little later, not move him in the least? She snatched a furtive glimpse at him sitting straight and stern beside her, his arms still folded, his lips still in that grim, set line, and his eyes, his *unbelieving* eyes on the floor.

The sermon that followed was most impressive. At the very first word Aunt Faith knew that Barry's interest was aroused, and that he gave respectful attention to every point. Yet he was like one standing at the top of an amphitheater where an acrobatic entertainment was going on in which he had no personal interest. His mind was assenting to the points made, his sense of humor pleased by several witty stories, his superficial admiration stirred by the personality and magnetism of the speaker, but he himself was miles away from the whole subject that was being discussed, as if it were a thing he had settled long ago as not for him.

Gradually Aunt Faith sensed all this, and knew in some degree what her sister had meant when she sighed and was worried about her eldest boy. And so, quietly, she went on praying. She could not fathom the reason why Barry should be this way. Only the adversary and God knew. Only the Holy Spirit could help here, she was sure, no matter what the cause had been. So she prayed.

At the end of the sermon an invitation was given for all who would accept Christ to come forward, and many came. Barry sat with folded arms leaning over the balcony rail and watched all who went forward, but still with that same sneer on his lips, those same unbelieving eyes. At the very end an old man sitting in the last seat, with the marks of sin on his face, came hesitantly out into the aisle and tottered up to the front. Barry watched him all the way. When he was just opposite where he sat, Barry said in a clear, amused tone: "*Humph!* He won't last long!"

Barry was courteous at the end, greeting old friends, introducing new ones, and they had a pleasant talk.

Then they went out to the car.

"How about a little spin in the moonlight before we go home, Aunt Faith?" Barry asked gaily. "The folks won't be home till all hours. They always stay till the last cat's hung. I'd like to show you the new tennis courts in the park and the fountains and sunken gardens. It's swell out there!"

"Why, yes, I'd enjoy a ride," smiled Aunt Faith.

So they drove about the park and Barry showed her all the changes that had come since she went away. Then he took her a little way out the highway past the new estates. But underneath her apparent interest in what was being said his aunt kept feeling that this was the time, the opportunity that Barry's mother had hoped she would have, yet her lips were dumb. God gave her nothing to say to this dear boy who had wandered away. What was the reason? If those inspiring songs, the testimonies, the prayers, and that wonderful sermon had not reached him, what could she say?

At last they drove back home. When they got to the house they found the children were there ahead of them. They were having an altercation about the radio and their voices were loud and angry.

"I think you're awful mean, Steve! I don't care if you do want to get XYZ. I was here *first*, and I want to hear the Jubilee singers. It's just time for them to begin!" Joy was saying petulantly, and she stamped her small foot furiously at her brother and snatched at his arm.

"Aw, shut up, cantcha!" said the brother. "I wantta get the time. Cantcha see I'm setting my watch? Look out there! Let that dial alone, you little pest, you!" And suddenly Steve gave Joy a resounding slap on her round pink cheek.

"You horrid mean thing!" screamed Joy, and broke into tempestuous sobs. "I'm going to tell Mother!"

"All right, tell her! And I'll tell Dad! You know

what *he*'ll say. I'm required to set my watch at night or I'll get a bawling out for being late to breakfast! There he comes now. Dad, this kid won't let me get the right time on the radio—!"

"Mother! Steve's spoiling the Jubilee singers and you said I could stay up till they were done singing."

But the father and mother were engaged in an argument and didn't hear them.

"Myra, I tell you you are utterly mistaken. That woman's name is Bartlett, not Brown, and she lives on Second Street."

"It is *not*, it's *Brown!*" declared Myra angrily. "She just told me her name! And the woman with her is her sister. They've just moved here from Buffalo and they're in awful trouble."

"No, her name is Bartlett!" insisted the minister. "I guess I know my own church members! You probably misunderstood her."

"I did *not* misunderstand her! I guess I have as good sense as you have, and I'm not in the least deaf! They've just moved here from Buffalo and her husband is dead."

"Oh no, he isn't dead at all. I tell you I know that woman. She's always in some uncomfortable position and wants help. In fact I called on her the other day and found she'd gone on a picnic. The woman who was with her lives next door to her and she called out to me that she had gone on a picnic."

"John! You are the most exasperating man! It's you who have got things mixed. That woman's name is Brown. She just told me so, and the younger one is her sister, Jane Hawkins, who lives with her. I had a long talk with them before I endeavored to get you to come and speak with them. They wanted to see you and talk with you! They are in great trouble!"

"But, my dear, you saw that I was busy with Mr. Merchant. You must have seen that I was engaged in a most important conversation. I simply couldn't turn away from him to talk with people whom I can see any day. Besides, I'm sure you are mistaken. Those women live down on Second Street!"

"They certainly do not," said the minister's wife, two red spots coming out on her cheeks and making her look in her anger a little like her pretty daughter Rosalie. "You seem to think I have no brains nor ears. Didn't I tell you they told me their names? They said—"

"But my dear, what does it matter what their names are? I tell you I was engaged in a most important conversation. Mr. Merchant was telling me that the minister over in the Second church has been criticizing our methods over here. He says that we are not strictly fundamental, and he's having meetings himself in his own church, beginning next week. He's having that evangelist that talks about himself so much, and *yet* he criticizes *us!* You can see that it was most important that I understand thoroughly the whole matter!"

"*Why*, I should like to know?" snapped his wife. "And what earthly difference does it make what that other minister thinks, anyway? He's not orthodox himself! Besides, John, I think he has put himself in a position where any decent self-respecting man shouldn't even speak to him on the street. Do you know what he told Betty Asher? He told her it was perfectly right for her to get a divorce if she wanted to, *and marry again,* too! And they say that he doesn't approve of foreign missions either! I declare I don't see why you pay the slightest attention to what he says."

"Mother!" howled Joy. "Steve's pulling my hair!"

"I was not, you little pest, you!"

But the mother and father went on arguing and didn't hear.

Barry led Aunt Faith into the library, but the twins were ahead of them, having entered from the pantry where they had been rifling the cake box. They had large pieces of chocolate cake in their hands and were wrangling at the top of their voices.

"I don't see why you can't lend me your new hat to wear tomorrow," said Jean. "You hardly ever wear it, and it's awfully becoming to me. You know I haven't a hat fit to wear to call on those young people at the hotel. They promised to go to church tomorrow night if I came for them. I don't see why you have to be so stingy with your old hat anyway. You are always so terribly mine-and-thine about your things."

"Just because you ruin everything you get, and then come back on me for mine!" said Joan sticking up her chin disagreeably. "You had a new hat at the same time I had mine, and you chose to wear it to the picnic in the rain and get it all out of shape. Now you want to spoil mine! You shan't have mine to slam around!"

"You know that isn't so, Joan Kent! Look at the dress I'm wearing. There isn't a spot on it and yours has had to be cleaned twice, and they were bought at the same time! Besides, what's a hat? It will be all out of fashion before another season. It's an awfully odd shape anyway, and not at all your style. It doesn't become you *in the least!*"

"It does so, it's the most becoming hat I ever had, and if you don't like it why do you want to borrow it? Nothing doing! I'm taking care of my hat, and anyway I hate the idea of people thinking we wear each other's things just because we're twins. Mother, speak to Jean, won't you, and tell her she can't have my hat? She's spoiled her own, and now she wants mine!"

"Mother, won't you tell Joan she's *got* to let me borrow her hat just once? I haven't any hat fit to wear with my new dress to the hotel after those swell New York girls."

But the mother and father were still arguing and didn't hear.

Just then Rosalie and John came in, and Rosalie went straight over to her father and interrupted him, laying her hand on his arm.

"Dad, what do you think?" she said, her eyes very bright and her cheeks as pink as if they had been painted. "Mrs. Cromwell, the lady who lives in that big new estate up the highway, was in the meeting tonight, and she heard me sing that solo in the anthem, and liked it so much she's asked me to sing at her garden party next month! Isn't that perfectly wonderful!"

"Aw, *you!* You think you have a *voice!*" sneered her brother John. "You hit at least three sour notes tonight!"

"Sez *you!*" flashed Rosalie, lifting her chin, anger snapping in her eyes. "What do *you* know about music? You think because you can strum on the guitar that you can criticize everybody! You can't tell a sour note from a sweet one. I can tell you I get mighty sick of your everlasting strumming on those old twangy strings. Keeping us awake at night and waking us up in the morning. What in the world you ever took up that instrument for, I don't see. It's no earthly good to anybody! Just so you can sit there by the hour and roll your eyes and sing silly love songs. If you'd get a real instrument and take lessons you might someday be in a position to tell a sour note from a sweet one, but at present your opinion isn't worth much."

"Well, I wasn't the only one who thought so," said John with a superior smile. "That Mr. Grant and his simpering wife were laughing at you. They've studied at some conservatory or other, and every time you sang that high G or C or whatever you call it, your voice went sour, and they laughed! All righty! You can turn up your nose, and you can go right on singing in public and making a fool of yourself if you want to, singing *sour* notes if you don't know the difference. But don't flatter yourself people enjoy it! That Mrs. Cromwell is no musician if she thought you sang beautifully. *Not me!* You just spoiled the whole service for me! *My sister* singing *sour notes!* I wished the floor would open and let me through. I was *ashamed* of you, and *that's the truth!*"

"Oh, *shut up!*" said Rosalie in a loud angry voice.

And then came a wild hysterical sob from little Joy on the stairs:

"Mother! Steve *is* pulling my hair!"

"I wasn't pulling your hair!" snarled Steve, coming down the steps with an angry thump.

Suddenly Barry, who had come back into the hall and was standing in the doorway, began to sing in a high, sweet tenor:

I have the peace that passeth understanding,
 Down in my heart,
Down in my heart, down in my heart,
 I have the peace that passeth understanding,
Down in my heart,
 Down in my heart to stay!

He sang it all the way through amid an awful silence! Everyone in the room knew exactly what he meant. Even little Joy up there on the stairs, with two great tears rolling down her round pink cheeks, and two more just ready to follow, and her mouth open for another howl, stopped short and stared at him. Little Joy had been praying for Barry, and now she suddenly saw how she had been undoing her prayers by her actions here at home.

They all knew.

It was as if the words they had just been speaking were up there in the top of the room pointing down at them, accusing, condemning them. They could almost hear the echo of their angry voices lingering on the air. They listened to Barry with startled, horrified eyes, their faces growing white and shamed. They looked at the merry, worldly face of their brother as he sang and were condemned. They knew the witness of their lives before this unbelieving brother had belied the words they had spoken from their eager hearts in church.

The mother stood aghast, incredulous. Could it be that such little everyday homely contacts as this had led Barry away from God?

Steve, as he stood behind the big overstuffed chair, understood, and the words of the song went deep into his heart. He could still hear his own raucous voice calling his little sister names. Slowly his lashes drooped as the song went on, his gaze went down, his head bowed, he sank down lower and lower out of sight, till he was sitting on the floor with his face against the plush of the chair.

It was as if all around that room there was a panorama of the acts and words of that family, especially during the last few weeks while the evangelist had been with them, and they had all been working to save souls!

John, standing in front of the big back window, suddenly and silently turned himself about, and catching the heavy crimson curtains one in each hand, he brought them quietly together behind his back, obliterating himself; he stood there gazing into the darkness of the backyard seeing himself as God must see him, for the first time in his life.

The twins had giggled when Barry first began to sing, then they looked at each other with shamed glances, their eyes fell, and they silently turned and slowly melted out of the room into the dark dining room.

Rosalie blanched and stared at Barry wide-eyed. For underneath all her silliness and foolish pride and conceit, Rosalie was real, and she truly wanted Barry to come back to God. She had been earnestly praying for him every day. And now she saw how her own words and actions had led him astray, and her heart was filled with deep remorse and sorrow.

But it was the gray-haired father most of all who winced at that song. He had given his life to the service of God and longed more than anything else to be able to lead people to the Lord Jesus Christ, and now he saw how in the little daily contacts of life he had been leading his beloved eldest son away from Christ.

He had come to stand by the mantel, with his elbow on the shelf and his head bowed on his hand, while that song was going on, and when it was finished he lifted his head and looked at Barry.

"That's the way we've looked to you, Barry! That's the way we've been!" he said in a tone of deep sorrow.

"Oh, *Dad!*" said Barry, suddenly apologetic, "I was only *kidding!*"

"Yes, but it was true!" said the father. "That's the way we've been. That's what we have done! And you've made us see ourselves!"

And then as if the Lord had suddenly come into the room, the gray-haired father turned and began to talk to God.

"Oh, Lord," he said slowly, his hands clasped before him as he looked up, while the family stood petrified and listened. "Oh, Lord, *I've sinned!* We've *all* sinned! But *I* most of all. And now I'm glad you've sent me word about it. Lord, I didn't know I was doing that! But now, Lord, I can't do anything about it myself. It's an awful habit that I didn't realize, and by myself I can't cure it. But—I'm handing over my sinful self to you now, to be put to death daily. Do it *now*, Lord, at *any cost*, and live the life of my Lord in me, that others may see thee and not myself in me!"

With broken heart, the gray-haired father went down upon his knees beside the big chair to pray half the night.

And one by one the family stole shamedly up the stairs to their rooms, to meet their conscience and their God. Till only Barry was left, standing in the doorway, looking with misty eyes at his father, listening as his father confessed his sins aloud to God!

"*Dad!*" he said in a husky, choking voice, "it was only a *joke!* I didn't mean a thing!"

But his father was talking aloud to God and didn't hear.

"Dad! *Oh, Dad!*"

Then suddenly Barry turned, brushing away a quick tear, and with a last lingering look at his father kneeling there, he strode up the stairs to his room, to meet *his* conscience and *his God!*

And up in the guest room Aunt Faith was kneeling by her bed, thanking God that the Holy Spirit has ways of working that mortals may not use.

THE OLD GUARD

MRS. Dunlap, Mrs. Bryan, and Miss Dewy arrived at the church fifteen minutes before the appointed hour for the missionary meeting. It was their custom to do so. Until a few months ago there had been four of them, but God had called the fourth one, Mrs. Bonner, first to be laid low on a bed of sickness and then, just six weeks ago, to go home to him. Mrs. Bonner had been their leader, and for many years the president of their society. She had been a slim, sweet, fair little woman with a consecrated mind, body, and fortune, and gifted with the power of leadership to an extraordinary degree.

Even while she lay sweetly, uncomplainingly upon her bed, in what they all knew was her last illness, the power of her consecrated life had gone out almost as when she walked among them. Her Christianity was vital and held them like a magnet. Even the worldly church members acknowledged her gentle but firm leadership and followed where she led, at least from afar.

Miss Dewy was short and sharp-tongued, keen, quick-tempered, and sarcastic, but she loved her Lord devotedly. She shed many tears and spent many hours of earnest prayer over her own short-comings, but she had been known to tell a fellow member exactly how she thought that member looked to the eyes of God, offending her beyond reparation, and then to agonize in prayer for her all night long.

Mrs. Bryan was a meek, quiet little creature with prematurely gray hair and chastened eyes, but a faith in God and a power in prayer that stopped at nothing. She had seen much sorrow in her life but had let it bring forth the fruit of righteousness. She wore plain clothes and gave astonishingly to missions. People ignored her except when there was hard work to be done, and then they hunted her up and said it was "so good of her to be willing." Somehow she could always find time to visit the poor and the sick, and could usually produce many partly worn garments for people who needed them.

Mrs. Dunlap was a hard-working woman with a crippled son to support and a way of leaning hard upon God. She had seen better days and was well educated, having acquired a deep culture which her hard work had not eradicated.

All three of these women believed with all their hearts in prayer.

They had met often with Mrs. Bonner, even during her last illness, to pray for their beloved church and missionary society. And now, even since Mrs. Bonner was gone, they carried on. They came early to the meetings to pray. They had no other convenient place to meet.

The women in the church who knew about it thought it strange of them. They felt somehow rebuked when they came upon them in prayer. "Just without any reason at all!" they said in vexed tones, backing out of the vestibule to wait till the devotions were over. "*Just* to *pray!* How odd of them!" They called them "The Old Guard" and laughed a little derisively. Presently the name got around among the women of the church, "The Old Guard!"

The Old Guard entered the dim quiet of the ladies' parlor and went straight to the sacred corner where they had brought so many perplexing problems in the past to the Throne of Grace, and prayed them through. There they knelt in their accustomed corner and began to talk to God. Their hearts were heavily burdened for their dear society, yet there was a ring of triumph and thanksgiving to their opening words. They had to thank God first for the way everything had worked out, for just the night before, the session of the church had formally approved the appointing of Mary Lee to go to India as their own special missionary.

Of course it had been rather expected for the last three years while Mary Lee, under the patronage of Mrs. Bonner, had been completing her course at Bible school with that in mind. But now that Mrs. Bonner was gone, the Old Guard had greatly feared that the church might lose interest in that project which had been so dear to Mrs. Bonner's heart.

Therefore, thanksgiving about Mary Lee had been first on their lips in the prayers they uttered. And after that, less jubilantly, there was tender prayer for the new president of the society, Mrs. Lansing Searle. She was to take charge that day for the first time, and in proportion as these good women feared for her ability to take the place of the sainted Mrs. Bonner, so they waited on the Lord in prayer that he might endue her with wisdom from above. It was not their votes that had made Mrs. Searle president; but the majority of the members were intrigued by having a woman of such wealth and social prominence among them, and the Old Guard had been outvoted.

Mrs. Lansing Searle was pretty and popular. She had honey-colored hair, most appealing eyes, a firm little red mouth, and wore orchid costumes. The name wasn't hyphenated, but her friends always spoke it as if it were, rhythmically, Mrs. *Lansing*-Searle, as if any other Searle were not worth mentioning. She was small and gentle-looking, and one couldn't imagine that she would be anything but a figurehead. But she had an amazingly stubborn chin, and tight little lips that could sneer. Mrs. Dunlap's crippled son, who had uncanny insight into character even from his invalid chair by the street window, said she was the devil's best counterfeit of a saint. Of course, Chester Dunlap himself was not yet sanctified in his own life. But so, all the more Chester Dunlap's mother laid the new missionary society president in the care of the Almighty and pled for her soul. It is to be hoped that Mrs. Lansing Searle would not have laughed had she heard that prayer. For the Old Guard had laid aside their prejudices and their preconceived fears, and were praying as if their very life, and the life of the missionary society, depended upon it—as perhaps it did.

The three dear souls had got so far into communion with the other world as to have lost their fears and dropped their burdens again and had gone back to climax their prayers with another little paean of joy about Mary Lee and India, when Mrs. Appleby and a flock of followers arrived unaccustomedly in the vestibule and paused an instant to look around. Mrs. Appleby was the new vice-president. She was large and well-groomed, with a baby complexion, perfect teeth, and big fat pearls in her ears. Her costume reminded one of a flourishing apple tree in blossom, green with a touch of rose about her hat, exceedingly smart. Jerome Appleby, her husband, was a great clubman.

"Let's see, girls, which door goes into the Ladies' Parlor? This one? I declare I don't know my way around here!" she babbled, and then with her followers boomed into the quiet hush where prayer pervaded the atmosphere.

"My soul! Is there something going on here already? We can't be late!" she blustered noisily.

"Sh! There's someone praying!" whispered Mrs. Melton, who was always afraid of doing the wrong thing.

"It's only the Old Guard," giggled young Mrs. Stacey in an ill-suppressed whisper. "My word!

Wouldn't you think they'd have the politeness to wait till the new president arrives to open the meeting?"

The soft voice of prayer in the corner dropped into a quiet amen, and the three devoted women arose and took their seats, not even looking the indignation that mortal Christian women could scarce help feeling.

The huddled invaders of the holy place stood uncertainly by the door conversing in subdued tones, a trifle awed, perhaps even a little shamed by the dignity of those three quiet backs. A moment later Mrs. Lansing Searle entered gaily with a trilling laugh to her companion. She gave a quick searching glance around, taking in the Old Guard without seeming to do so, and then, assuming a gentle attitude of superiority, went forward to the desk and took her place with much self-possession—just as though she had always been president of that society; just as though this was not the very first time she had ever had anything to do with a missionary society.

Of course she was a clubwoman. She had a reputation for being one of the best parliamentarians in town. She could recite Roberts' Rules of Order from start to finish, and she could make a charming and graceful speech. These had been qualifications for the position intensively urged at her election.

After she had arranged her notebook and a few papers she had brought with her on the desk, and glanced at her trinket of a wristwatch, she signaled to the piano one of the frivolous young women who had arrived in her company, and who, obviously, was not a frequenter of missionary meetings. Then she looked around with a smile.

"Ladies, will you please come to order?" she said, although there was not the slightest sign of disorder in the room.

The group around Mrs. Appleby came about-face and selected seats in the shadows near the rear.

"Let us open the meeting by singing number two seventy-three," announced the president in a clear voice after having consulted the bit of paper on the desk.

Now Mrs. Lansing Searle was not familiar with hymnology, neither did her home contain any very great selection of hymnbooks, but the women who had so earnestly engineered her election to the office of president because they wished to secure her influence and social standing for their church, had carefully supplied her with one of the church hymnals and it had reposed on top of the piano in her home all week. At the very last minute while she was powdering her nose and putting on her scrap of a hat, she had remembered it and called to her young daughter Edwina.

"Darling, won't you run down and pick me out a couple of hymns for that meeting I'm to lead this afternoon? I forgot all about it. Get good old ones that everybody knows."

So Edwina had carefully selected "Nearer, My God, to Thee" and "Onward Christian Soldiers" and written their numbers into her mother's neat program.

But the janitor had unfortunately forgotten to gather up the hymnbooks from the Christian Endeavor rally held the night before, in order to distribute the church hymnals which the missionary society always used. So it was not the good old staid hymnbook that the ladies reached for, fluttering the leaves to find number two seventy-three, but a cheery little gospel songbook.

However, the majority of ladies present were utterly new to the ways of this missionary society, and willingly began to sing the rousing old song, "Hold the Fort." Even Mrs. Searle was none the wiser, for she had left her own book at home on the piano, and so quite cheerfully entered into the song:

Ho my comrades, see the signal waving in the sky!
Reinforcements now appearing, Victory is nigh.

The new president sang her satisfaction in the selection and thought how keen her Edwina was to select so appropriate a song, although the tune did seem a bit odd. But, reinforcements! Who, but herself and the bright new friends she had brought into this dull old society to give it new life, were the reinforcements? She let out her cultured voice in full power on "Hold the fort for I am coming!" and "waved the answer back to heaven" with great gusto: "By thy grace *we will!*" without a thought of him by whose grace alone they could possibly hope to win. She was only exulting in what an appropriate selection Edwina had found.

But by the time the second verse was reached, her attention was called to the outer door, which swung back just as Mrs. Cresswell Kingdon entered in all the glory of a new black satin spring costume. She wore long jet earrings dangling on her shoulders, and her sharp, haughty face was flushed with brick-colored rouge, in a sort of permanent flush. She was followed by nine other smartly attired women. Here at last was the important contingent! Mrs. Searle had been afraid they were going to fail her after all.

The room was fairly filled with quiet elderly women now, the regular old members of the missionary society scattered here and there among the people who were to give new life to them, looking a bit like barnyard fowls among the peacocks. But when Mrs. Cresswell Kingdon entered with her friends, a little stir of surprise and something almost like fear entered the old ranks of faithful ones.

They came in noisily, breezily, almost as if they were amused at themselves for being there, but Mrs. Searle smiled complacently and opened her voice to sing its best as they advanced toward the front seats.

"See the mighty host advancing!" sang the ladies earnestly, "Satan leading on!"

Mrs. Dunlap looked up suddenly and saw Mrs. Cresswell Kingdon leading her troop of society ladies and suddenly put down her head and put up her handkerchief to cover a smile. She lived in too close touch with her irreverent, fun-loving son not to see the humorous side of things. But nobody else saw it, and least of all the new president who was still reflecting on Edwina's perspicacity.

When the song was ended Mrs. Lansing Searle readjusted her papers, and with as much self-possession as she had ever used in presiding over a club meeting, she said:

"Let us pray!"

She selected obviously the second of the papers that lay on her desk, spread it before her, and without any attempt to close her eyes she read her prayer in a pleasant conversational tone.

"Lord, we thank thee today that there are so many gifted people here who are willing to devote their time and their talents and their ability to building up thy kingdom. We feel sure that thou wilt bless our plans for making the world better, and wilt bring great good out of this little meeting today. We know that a little leaven leaveneth the whole lump, and so our efforts here, though begun in a small way, will presently increase and cover the whole earth, and thy kingdom shall at length come on earth through our efforts. Amen."

Mrs. Dunlap heard Persis Dewy draw her breath in a quick little breath of protest at the word about leaven being compared to good. She began to pray softly that Persis would not feel that she must jump right up after the prayer and enlighten the new president, telling her that leaven always stood for evil in the Bible, never for good. It would be like Persis to do that in her eagerness to instruct everybody in the dispensational truth in which she was so much interested.

But the new president gave Persis Dewy no time

to spoil her Christian testimony with her sarcastic little tongue. The devotional ceremony being thus glibly disposed of by a hymn and a prayer, she hastened on to the business of the hour.

"Ladies," she said sweetly, "I want to thank you for the honor you have done me in making me your president, and I intend to take this office over conscientiously and do my very best for you. I have been informed that the society has been somewhat vegetating during the illness of our dear Mrs. Bonner, for naturally while she was laid aside she was not able to keep up with the times. We must not blame her for that. She did her best, I am sure, and we are all so glad that she is free from pain and has passed to her reward.

"But now, ladies, I am sure you all feel with me that we must get to work promptly and bring things up to date. And to that end I have invited in some new members who will be glad to help us reconstruct things. I have talked over plans with some of them and find them quite willing to work, and they really have some charming ideas. I know you will be delighted with them when you hear them. But now the first thing is to get these people signed up so that they can help us vote on all the questions that come up. Mrs. Archer, our new secretary, unfortunately could not be present today as she had a previous engagement, so I will appoint Miss Dewy, the former secretary, to be secretary pro tem. Miss Dewy, will you just take the names of the new members? Mrs. Appleby, you are our new treasurer, will you kindly follow Miss Dewy around and take the dues? A dollar and a half each, isn't it? Yes, I thought I was right."

Persis Dewy, grim and wrathy, arose with her roll book and started out among the elite, grudgingly allowing them to write their names under the beloved names of saintly members of the past. It seemed to her a desecration. But one could not refuse to accept new members to a missionary society. And nearly all those present were members of the church. What could she do? She resented the fact that these rich, worldly women were being brought into the society to bolster up the funds of the organization. She very much doubted the wisdom of raising money by any such strategy. She did not feel that the Lord would be pleased with money acquired in this way. But she had just been praying with the Old Guard that the Lord might have his way in her, and she knew that the Lord would not let one of his own plans be frustrated, so she went about with her book and held her peace.

There was a little stir in the meeting, some laughing and talking among the new people, a bit of banter among the younger ones. The old members looked about a trifle worried. It did not seem like the usual atmosphere of their precious meeting which they had always so enjoyed in Mrs. Bonner's day. But it was soon over, and Mrs. Lansing Searle sailed into the preliminaries of the business of the day, showing great skill and prowess, as well as an intimate knowledge of the details of the society that had been placed under her control. The quiet, meek members who had heretofore gone with fear and trembling through the intricacies of motions and secondings, and had taken their votings seriously with due consideration, now found themselves so hustled from one point to another that they were almost mentally out of breath. They presently arrived at the crux of the matter, the real reason for this meeting, which was Mary Lee and the matter of arranging for her support as the church's own special missionary in India.

The president glided smoothly from the old business to the matter of deepest interest to them all, saying that they had come together to consider the matter of sending a special missionary from the church to some foreign point to "elevate and uplift humanity," but she said not one word about Mary Lee. And it was almost time for Mary Lee to arrive! Could it be possible that Mrs. Lansing Searle had not been informed that she was coming to speak to them?

At last Mrs. Dunlap arose, taking advantage of the president's brief pause for breath, and dared to interrupt.

"Madam President," she said, and her cultured voice drew instant attention, even from the new members whom the president had commandeered. It had always been a source of annoyance to Mrs. Lansing Searle whenever she had given enough attention to the woman to think about her at all, that Mrs. Dunlap should possess such a cultured voice in spite of her shabby clothes.

"Madam President, pardon me for interrupting,"

went on the cultured voice, "but I wasn't sure whether anyone had told you that we are to have the pleasure of a few words from our missionary, Miss Mary Lee herself, this afternoon. I thought I would mention it before she comes in. She is due to arrive almost any minute now and will have to talk as soon as she comes because she has only a brief time and must hurry away."

"Oh *really*?" said Mrs. Searle with a lifting of her eyebrows and a quality in her tone that small boys use when they say, "Oh *yeah?*" "But my dear Mrs. Dunlap, that won't be necessary at this time. We might have the janitor telephone her not to come if you know the address. We really haven't time for anything like that this afternoon. We have important business to transact and these ladies," with a swift glance toward the smart group of newcomers, "have given us their important time to come and help us. They are very busy women, you know, and have engagements every hour in the day."

Mrs. Searle smiled as if that settled the question.

But Mrs. Dunlap, with the sternness of a prophet of old, held her ground.

"You don't understand, Mrs. Searle. This has all been arranged for. Mrs. Bonner herself saw to it before she died that Mary Lee should have permission to get away from her afternoon class in the Bible school where examinations are now going on for the end of the term. It was to have been Mrs. Bonner's surprise for her beloved society, and she took great pleasure in feeling that though she could not be here herself she could have a little part in planning this meeting. And—" as the vestibule door swung wide letting in a young girl with sweet eyes and a quiet manner, "here comes Mary Lee now! She can take only a very few minutes, and she was promised that she could speak at once. Come right up front, Mary Lee! We know you haven't much time to spare, and we're just so glad to see you and have a few words from our very own missionary. Ladies, this is Mary Lee, who is going out to India shortly to preach the gospel for us."

Oh, Mrs. Dunlap knew very well she was being officious, but what else could she do? As she sat down and Mary Lee came smiling to the front there was a feeble applause from the old quiet members of the society, ending in a painful questioning sound, as if perhaps they had not done the right thing.

The new contingent simply sat and stared at this plainly dressed, flower-faced girl who stepped to the front, gave a lovely smile to the haughty president, and began to speak at once:

"Dear friends, I am so glad to have this chance to thank you all for giving me the opportunity to go and tell the story of salvation to a people who have never heard of Jesus Christ their Savior.

"It was five years ago that I discovered Jesus Christ to be *my* Savior. I was brought up, as you know, in a Christian home. I went to church and Sunday school. I even taught a Sunday school class, but I was not a Christian myself until five years ago. I was not saved! I did not think I needed to be saved. I thought I was quite good enough for God's standards.

"As I look back on that time I see now that I was in just the same situation as the people in India to whom I am going. So many of them do not feel the need of a Savior from *sin*.

"But God had to show me that I was utterly sinful through and through according to his standards. It was a bitter knowledge that I had to learn, that I was not one whit better in any way or more fit to stand before him than any so-called heathen. It was when I saw myself like that, as a sinner, that I cried out to God and he showed me Jesus Christ as my Savior. I saw my Lord hanging there on the cross for me. I knew it was my sins that had nailed him there. And ever since then I have wanted to take to others the glad news that there is a Savior who has taken away the sin of the world, a Savior who is able to *keep* those that put their trust in him.

"I tell you this today so that you may know why I am going out to the far field in India. And I know that I am not going uselessly nor foolishly, for the Savior that I take to them is able to save souls and 'there is none other name under heaven given among men whereby we must be saved.'

"It is a delight to me to look into your faces this afternoon. I shall remember you all when I am far away and it will be sweet to know that you are praying for me and loving the work as much as I. Because, you know, it is *your* work. Through sending me out there you yourselves are really leading those people for whom Jesus died, to know him, 'whom to know is life eternal.'

"I thank you all for letting me say these few words

to you and I hope I'll know you better before I actually go." Her eyes rested fleetingly, almost questioningly, upon Mrs. Cresswell Kingdon, who sat frowning in amazed disapproval behind her brick-red rouge. "Now I'm sure you will excuse me, for I must hurry right back to my class."

Mary Lee smiled shyly and went swiftly down the aisle and out the door amid an awkward silence that lasted till the door had swung behind her.

It wasn't the kind of reception that Mrs. Bonner had planned for the girl who was so dear to her heart and whom she had been helping to fit for her great work abroad. The hearts of the Old Guard were boiling with shame and indignation, but there wasn't a thing they could have done about it. It was Mrs. Searle's place to give this girl a few words of welcome at the very least. But no, they had let her walk away, and though she was just modest Mary Lee and thought very little of herself, she could not help but sense the coldness in that meeting.

Mrs. Bryan wiped away a few futile tears, Mrs. Dunlap sat sternly fixing the new president with an anguished eye of reproof, and Miss Dewy's little earnest face simply boiled with righteous rage. But the new president was utterly oblivious. She stood haughtily in her orchid robes like an offended princess, and then smiled a slow, amused, contemptuous smile toward her own friends.

"Well, really! Quite an unexpected innovation!" She laughed lightly and murmured: "Oh, well, not *much* time lost!" with a glance at her watch.

The Old Guard sat unsmiling, with downcast eyes,

trying to pray, trembling in their souls. The rest of the former members didn't quite know what it was all about, but sensed a hostile attitude, sat timidly on the fence, so to speak, and waited to see what the outcome would be.

"Now, ladies, to return to essentials," laughed the president, tapping lightly with a gold pencil on the desk, "you will please come to order. I believe we are ready for business again. And before we go any further I am going to ask one of our new members to tell us something of a plan she has been hearing about. It will, I think, give us an entirely new vision of what missionary work should be, and create new impetus to work for it. I have some delightful plans which I shall unfold to you when you have heard Mrs. Kingdon speak. Mrs. Kingdon has recently attended a large mass meeting in New York where the ideas she has to offer were brought forward, and from all I hear it is the beginning of a new era in church missions. Mrs. Kingdon, will you tell us all that you have told me?"

Then up rose Mrs. Kingdon, the permanent flush on her cheeks, and the dangling glitter of her earrings somehow out of keeping with all ideas of a missionary meeting. But Mrs. Kingdon did not seem at all embarrassed to be addressing such a body. She arose briskly with an air of knowing about everything, and began to speak.

"Ladies, this is the first time I have ever been in a missionary meeting in my life! Missions have never appealed to me before. But I have been glad to learn recently that missions as a whole have taken a new turn, new methods are entering in, new standards being raised, and I have come to feel that missions under the new conditions can be made quite worthwhile.

"I do not know whether or not you are all aware that there have been recent investigations into mission work abroad. Some startling facts have been brought to light which have made a few brave souls who have done the investigating speak their minds. And there has not been lacking an eager response by many thinking women of today, who under the former regime held aloof from the efforts that were being put forth in a narrow and bigoted way to force dogmas upon a people who already had their own religion and resented having a new one forced upon them.

"We have no right to try to force our views upon others nor to say that there is but one way of salvation, whatever that term salvation may mean. I'm sure *I* don't know. We must look upon other nations as merely brothers in a common quest for truth and beauty and righteousness. Because some of us happen to believe in Jesus in our land is no reason why we should discount Buddha or Mohammed. We should learn to be tolerant, to live out the spirit of Jesus who went about doing good. We cannot do good to people whom we antagonize by trying to force some traditional dogmas and beliefs upon them. They have a right to their own religion. There is great danger, in the present mode of carrying on foreign mission work, of subordinating the educational to the religious objective. For that reason it is most important whom we send to the foreign field to represent us.

"You will pardon the personal reference, but it seems to me that we have had an illustration brought before us, in the words of the young girl who just attempted to make a speech. Such cant as that is most unfortunate! It is a specimen of what I have been talking about—theological dogma as an obsession. What possible good could such talk do the heathen? What they need is practical uplift! They need to be taught how to grow better crops, to have better homes, to understand and appreciate the beauties in life.

"With all due respect to dear Mrs. Bonner—and no one appreciates more than I all that she has done and sacrificed of her time and money and herself—yet she was behind the time! She was shut away so long by illness that she did not realize that the world had moved on beyond a mere fanatical belief in a tradition that no one who is at all up with the times could possibly accept. It seems to me, Madam President, that it would be most unfortunate in more ways than one if a girl like the one to whom we have just listened should be sent forth to represent our church. Narrow, ignorant, fanatical, and absolutely untrained, ranting of outgrown formulas! We are done with such things in this age of intelligence. Evangelism is no longer the way to reach the masses! The world wants practical help! It appeals for an eternal gospel emancipated from unalterable dogmas built around absurd theological doctrines, many of them long disproved; stereotyped patterns of doctrine and static phrases which have gone dead!"

The high-sounding phrases slipped from the thin, hard Kingdon lips with authority, almost with arrogance, and the gathering of zealous women, almost overpowered by the new voices that had so astonishingly joined their ranks, sat bewildered and blinked at this strange new teaching. Only the Old Guard really understood the full purport of the remarks and sat aghast, driven to quick silent prayer as the speaker swept on her devastating way.

"We are done with oral evangelism, the kind of missionary work which this Miss Lee, to whom we have been listening, evidently represents. Human service without any words at all is better than evangelism. Medical missions represent in themselves the essentials of the Christian enterprise. We need to help make people well and strong and to teach them how to plant their farms to advantage. Planting corn and potatoes in the best way is far more important than working on their emotions to make them believe something that only a small percentage of the world really accepts anymore."

Mrs. Dunlap was listening intently now, her kindly face flushed with excitement, her heart praying, "Oh God, teach us what to do, what to say, how to keep still, and to speak only at the right moment."

"And now," said Mrs. Cresswell Kingdon, "I want to say, before I introduce my helpers who are willing to go to work at once on this campaign of raising the money for the enterprise in hand, that I feel we should utterly put out of our minds any idea of sending out this untaught girl to whom we have just been listening. And I am not offering wholly destructive criticism. I have a lovely substitute in mind. She is a graduate of one of our great modern universities, holds a diploma from a well-known medical college, has had a full nurse's training, and has taken a two years' course in agriculture, as well as various minor cultural courses which would be of untold value in a foreign land. She is also an accomplished linguist and would easily acquire the language wherever she went. She has in addition a charming personality, being young and quite good looking. And it just happens that it would be possible for us to get her services because she has planned to spend at least four or five years in the Orient pursuing some research work for her university, and she could just as well do our work *on the side!* I felt we were in great luck when I heard it, and I went to her at once and secured an option on her services for our church. She has had several other openings brought to her attention, but she has promised to wait one week before she considers the others. Her mother is a very dear friend of mine and that, of course, is why we have the preference. Now, ladies, I simply want your ratification of this and I can secure her at once."

Suddenly Mrs. Ryder, a quiet, meek woman in an old-fashioned brown hat and a shabby suit arose in the row of seats across the aisle from the elegant Mrs. Kingdon and, facing toward her, said in a trembly voice, frightened half out of her timid senses: "Excuse me for interrupting, but *is she a Christian?*"

Mrs. Kingdon turned her brick-colored scorn upon

the woman and fairly withered her with a glance. Then she looked to the president for protection, this interruption being out of order, and met that small dignitary's amused smile. She echoed a smile on her own face that said: "Of course this woman doesn't know any better and it isn't worthwhile to flaunt parliamentary rules at her." Then she brought her glance back to the frightened questioner who was still standing, holding her own.

Mrs. Kingdon, with a contemptuous smile, stared at the interrupter from the toe of her shabby shoe to the crown of her antiquated hat and answered:

"I'm sure I don't know, my dear. We don't go around asking people personal questions like that, do we? But I suppose of course she is, since she knows the request comes from a church. She isn't a heathen, at any rate," and Mrs. Kingdon turned back to her waiting audience as if the matter were ended.

The subdued questioner slumped quickly into her seat with a troubled look in her eyes and subsided. Mrs. Kingdon went rapidly on to the finish.

"So, just to bring this matter to a quick conclusion," she said disagreeably, "I'll make the motion, Madam President, that we approve the appointment of Miss Ann Patricia Melville as our special missionary from our church."

But before she had time to sit down, and before the president could arrange her complacent little mouth to put the question, Mrs. Dunlap arose with dignity and, looking toward the desk, said: "Madam President, may I ask whether Mrs. Kingdon and the rest of the meeting know that the session have already appointed Miss Mary Lee as our missionary, at a special meeting held for that purpose last evening?"

There was a little stir in the room, especially among the old members, a lifting of brows, a look of relief on some faces, a nod here and there, a quick disapproving glance toward the strangers in the room, and then every eye was fastened on Mrs. Kingdon, who had turned her cold stare on Mrs. Dunlap.

But Mrs. Dunlap did not belong to the Old Guard for nothing. She was not afraid to look the elegant Mrs. Kingdon in the eye as calmly as that lady herself could look. So after an instant Mrs. Kingdon's look melted into amusement. She shrugged her shoulders slightly and smiled toward Mrs. Searle.

"I fancy that it won't be hard to convince the session that they have made a mistake and need to rescind that action," she said calmly. "I'll be willing to undertake that personally. And now, ladies," she went on, ignoring Mrs. Dunlap, who was still standing and who by right had the floor, "suppose we go on and explain our plans a little farther before I put that motion. And to that end I want to introduce Mrs. Phil Wentworth. She has some delightful ideas which I'm sure you will enjoy."

Young Mrs. Wentworth arose with vivacity and, being immediately recognized by the chair, proceeded to unfold her plans.

"We have a perfectly thrilling play we are going to put on!" she said engagingly. "We've worked it all out, assigned the characters and everything, and we're going to be ready to produce it by the middle or last of next month. We're planning to sell tickets at a good price which will cover the full cost of production and net us at least a third of the sum required to carry out Mrs. Kingdon's plans. We shall expect every member of the society to be responsible for the sale of at least ten tickets, either selling them or paying for them herself. We have a very wonderful item to announce right at the start; we have secured the services of a professional trainer to get our play in shape, and a real live star herself to take the principal part in the play, so you can be assured that it will be a great success. It's a real thriller! I'm not going to tell you any more just now, but I'm sure that's enough to make you all wildly enthusiastic about selling the tickets!"

The young woman sat down amid a joyous patter of gloved hands and many smiles from the new contingent.

"And now let me introduce Mrs. Lola Duane," said Mrs. Kingdon quickly, before anyone else had a chance to interrupt. "She is the second of my delightful surprises."

Mrs. Lola Duane seemed a child barely out of high school. But in reality she was a youthful divorcee, daughter of a wealthy member of the church. She arose dimpling and lifting her long, effective lashes.

"And *I* am going to give a dance and bridge party combined," said Mrs. Duane, giving the meeting a glance that took them all into her confidence. "Isn't that going to be perfectly *darling?* I'm giving it at one of the large hotels so that we can have all the room we need. It's to be a costume dance for the young people, and a bridge party for the older ones. I'll tell you some of the unique features a little later when I have had time to get them all thought out perfectly. But *I* am going to be responsible for the *second* third of the money to send Miss Ann Patricia Melville to India, and we shall expect you all to be interested and try to further our plans, of course. It will be a subscription dance, and even if you can't come you can all buy tickets."

Mrs. Duane sat down amid more glove clapping and Mrs. Kingdon introduced her third assistant, Miss Charlotte Thayer, a well-tailored, perfectly groomed woman in her early forties.

"And *I* am going to give a progressive dinner!" said Miss Thayer in a throaty voice. "I have secured the loan of a large number of the handsomest homes in the city for our use on the evening selected, and we will have the fruit cup course at one house, the soup at another, the meat course at another, the salad at another, and the dessert at another. Some of these homes are the showplaces of the city and it will be a rare opportunity for those who have not the social entré into such homes to see the beautiful works of art which their more favored fellow citizens have gathered about them. We are charging enough for the tickets to cover taxi fare from one house to another. There will be minor details to be arranged later, but I am sure I have told you enough to make you exceedingly enthusiastic about rooting for this dinner. And *I* am going to be responsible for the *last* third of the money to send Miss Ann Patricia Melville to India!"

There arose quite a clamor of delight among the new members as Miss Thayer sat down, and for a moment the room was in a hubbub. Then the president tapped on her table for quiet.

"Ladies," she said, smiling like a rich donor who has just fed the children of the tenements, "I'm sure we are all very glad that these delightful people have come here today to interest themselves in the Lord's work and help so very practically toward the uplifting of the world. Now, wouldn't it be well to get right down to action? Mrs. Kingdon, will you repeat your motion which you made a little while ago before we were interrupted, so that everyone will understand?"

But before Mrs. Kingdon could get to her feet, Persis Dewy sprang up, her face white with anguish.

"Madam President," she said, her voice sharp in its intensity, "before such a motion is put to the meeting may I remind you all that we have a commission? And under our commission it would not be possible to even consider sending out a missionary who is not unquestionably a Christian with but one object, and that to preach Christ and him crucified as the only Savior from sin."

Persis Dewy paused for lack of breath, and Mrs. Searle, whose stare had been growing more and more coldly presidential, lifted her eyebrows inquiringly and said as sternly as her coral lips could frame the syllables, *"Commission?* I was not aware that we had a commission! Nobody informed me of any commission."

"It is printed right in our constitution." Miss Dewy's lips were trembling now. She had much ado to keep the tears from her eyes.

"Oh, *really?* But I don't happen to have a copy of the constitution. Won't you just read it to us, please, Miss Dewy?"

"Change the commission! Rewrite it!" called out Mrs. Kingdon in her hoarse voice. "That can easily be done afterward if we find it necessary. Madam President, I really think we ought to get this finished up. It is getting late and many of us have to leave in a few minutes."

"Just a minute, Mrs. Kingdon," said the president, trying to be diplomatic. "I really think we should get this matter clear and settled. Won't you read that commission, Miss Dewy?"

Miss Dewy had been fluttering through the pages of her secretary's book and now brought out a printed folder, and triumphantly stood up to read. Her voice rang out a challenge to the astonished little assembly: " 'Go ye into all the world and preach the gospel to every creature.'

" 'Thus it is written, and thus it behooved Christ to suffer and to rise from the dead the third day; and that repentance and remission of sins should be preached in his name among all nations, beginning at Jerusalem. And ye are witnesses of these things. . . .' "

Miss Dewy read the words impressively, and then, lifting earnest eyes, she broke into speech.

"Madam President, with a commission like that,

how could we send one out who could not witness that Christ had saved her soul? Christ did not say that we were to go into all the world and teach all nations to plant potatoes or corn. Those things of course would often be done by any Christian missionary, and have been done always, but they would be incidentals, not the object of going. Christ did not even say, 'Go ye into all the world and give medicine and heal the sick.' He said 'preach the gospel.'

"And how would one dare do what Mrs. Kingdon suggests—rewrite that commission? There is a curse pronounced upon anyone who dares to do that. It says:

" 'If any man shall add unto these things, God shall add unto him the plagues that are written in this book. And if any man shall take away from the words of the book of this prophecy, God shall take away his part out of the book of life, and out of the holy city, and from the things which are written in this book!' "

There was a frozen silence as Miss Dewy finished breathlessly. Suddenly Mrs. Kingdon arose.

"Madam President, I think the time has come to cut short such foolishness. Everybody knows that those are only verses from the Bible and quite antiquated. If Jesus were on the earth today it is sure he would never have spoken such narrow-minded words. The ideal Christ would be broader, more up-to-date. I have heard that there is a movement on foot to rewrite the Bible, and it does seem as if such a thing is needed, although of course I understand it is in traditionally lovely language and a few copies must be preserved as heirlooms. But if the Bible could be written today it would be quite a different matter. And we should never allow progress in great movements to be stopped by some little antiquated saying that was written in the days when wisdom and knowledge were in their very babyhood. I move, Madam President, that we return to the motion. Have I a second for it?"

"My dear," said the president, turning to Miss Dewy with a sweetly official smile, "those are only Bible verses, you know, and quite antiquated, not a commission that is binding upon us."

"But you don't understand," said Miss Dewy eagerly. "They are the words of Jesus Christ and were included in the constitution—we all signed our names to it. It reads, 'We, the undersigned, recognizing the above commission from our Lord and Master do solemnly pledge and band together—' That is the original page on which the charter members signed their names, Madam President, and we have at least twenty of those members present here this afternoon."

Mrs. Searle gave her an annoyed stare and then laughed outright.

"Well, dear me!" she said amusedly. "It seems there are other antiquated documents besides the Bible that we shall have to do away with before we can get on with really important matters. But, ladies, I certainly think that we need not hesitate to proceed with our business, in spite of this matter of the past that seems to be in the way. If we find afterward that it is necessary to reaffirm what we have done today with a second vote it will do no harm, and in the meantime we shall know just where we stand and can go forward with the work in hand without delay. I have no doubt that this document can easily be set aside. I will consult the session of the church. In the meantime, Mrs. Kingdon, will you kindly make that motion again? It is only a matter of raising the money quickly, you know, and of course we cannot afford to delay."

But before the lady in question could possibly get to her feet, the timid little Mrs. Ryder arose and spoke eagerly: "Madam President," she said, with an insistence in her voice that arrested the attention of everybody in the room. "I *must* say something! I had a little boy once. He was run over by an automobile. He knew he was going to die. He heard the doctor telling us, and he was afraid. Very much afraid! Then someone brought Miss Mary Lee to see him, and she told him about his Savior and the promise that he that believeth hath everlasting life. She talked gently and made him understand about it, and prayed with him, until he was happy and not afraid to die anymore because he was going to be with his Savior. And he told us he would be waiting for us in heaven, and he died happy. Mary Lee did that for my Johnny! That's why I want her to go as our missionary, and I promise to pray for her every day and give everything I can afford. But I could not vote for anyone to go out there to bring just education or agriculture, or even health to those people when they do not know the way of salvation." She fixed her earnest eyes on the annoyed president's face. "*You* might have to die, too, someday, Mrs. President! Would you want somebody to come and teach you how to make a better garden, or even how to keep your health when you weren't going to need it anymore? Wouldn't you want to know the way to heaven? No, I can't vote for any new kind of missionary society. I want the gospel of salvation sent to the uttermost parts of the earth, for other Johnnies, like my Johnny, who have to die. No, I couldn't vote for that other lady! I'd *have* to vote for *Mary Lee!*"

A gray look swept over Mrs. Searle's face as the woman spoke of dying, but she tried to laugh it off.

She lifted her hands with a helpless little gesture.

"Well, ladies," she said apologetically, "we seem to be up against prejudice. Perhaps it would be as well to let it all rest right here for today. After all, it's quite a matter of raising money. And if these good friends think they can get along without us, and raise the money it will take to send even a Mary Lee to India, let them try! We will give them one week! If they can by that time produce the needed amount for the whole year, why, let them do it, and we can go on and work somewhere where we are really needed. I think, however, a little judicious wire-pulling will bring this out all right. And I see no reason whatever why we should not go right on making our plans and securing our assistants, for undoubtedly when the elders of the church hear of this they will know how to explain it to our troubled friends, and make them understand what true progress is. It is always a little hard for *elderly* people to understand, but that is the way the world grows. Shall we just be dismissed now without ceremony? I promised that this meeting should close exactly at four o'clock, and it is now two minutes of four. Suppose we meet at this same time next week, when we shall hope for a better united understanding of the whole matter. Good afternoon!"

The new contingent drifted out on a breath of laughter, stirring up perfume of costly kind, dropping a light word here and there. Then the older members slid out quietly like frightened wraiths, hardly daring to look at one another, troubled in their minds, some of them still uncertain what it was all about, fearful that they might have sat too long on the fence.

The Old Guard came last, sadly, silently, walking together up the street far behind the rest, not noticed by the crowd that had dispersed in limousines, avoided even by the other old members who were troubled that they had not taken a more decided stand.

The Old Guard reached the Dunlap home, three rooms in a plain house, two bedrooms and a sitting-room-kitchen-and-dining-room in one. Chester, the crippled son, sat in the window watching them curiously as they entered. What had happened to bring sadness to his mother who had gone out so joyously a little while before?

Mrs. Dunlap led them into her own bedroom and without a word they knelt around her plain little bed and began to pray. Chester in the other room could hear them, and he brushed the mist from his eyes as the prayers went on.

They prayed, each of them, with a faith that

reached out and laid hold of the throne of God, and the two who did not live there went forth pledged to pray all night.

The next morning Miss Dewy went out early before her duties in the Public Library demanded her presence, and called upon various old members of the missionary society. And at noon instead of going to her lunch she called up more on the telephone. Late that afternoon they gathered by twos and threes at the home of one of the old members and had a prayer meeting. And the next day they met at another home and had another prayer meeting. Every day all that week they met to pray somewhere! And the last day every member who was alive and able to be out of bed was present!

And when the week was over they all hastened early to the church again, a half hour before the time set for the meeting.

But just as they were entering the door, Mrs. Ryder, the mother of Johnny who had died, came hurrying to join them, a light in her face.

"I have something to tell you," she said eagerly. "I have been baking gingerbread every day and selling it to get a little money together for today, and yesterday my husband came in while I was taking the last batch from the oven and wanted to know what I was doing. So I just told him all about it. He got interested, and asked a lot of questions about it. And by and by when we went up to bed he said, 'Lyddy, I'd like to send that Mary Lee out to India. How much does it cost?' 'Oh,' I said, 'John, it costs a great deal! It costs even a little more than the big stone you were going to put in the cemetery lot for our Johnny,' and I told him what we had to raise. He was still a long time and then he said: 'Lyddy, what say we just put plants on Johnny's grave another year or two and take the money we'd saved for that stone to send Mary Lee to India? Wouldn't our Johnny like it better to have Mary Lee in India teaching people how to die, than to have a big fine stone over him?' and I cried and said, 'Yes, John!' So we talked it over and I've brought the money! It won't be quite as much as we need, but I thought perhaps God would send the rest somehow."

And then each one opened her purse and took out her savings, and when they counted it there were *fifty dollars more* than they needed to send Mary Lee to India!

Down on their knees went the Old Guard, and all the faithful old members with them, and praised the Lord.

They were praising the Lord when the president and her satellites walked in, praising him in such clear ringing tones that the social interlopers paused in dismay, not knowing just how to break up a prayer and praise meeting like that! Not until Mrs. Kingdon walked in, and said in her hoarse voice: "For sweet pity's sake! Don't let's put up with any more sob-stuff. Let's get down to work!" And the president at her instigation announced a hymn. She hadn't remembered to look one up beforehand. She announced the first one the book opened to and sang away without having any idea how appropriate the words were.

*God moves in a mysterious way, his wonders to
   perform.
He plants his footsteps in the sea, and rides upon
   the storm.*

But the Old Guard sang fervently from the heart.

The routine business went through without a ripple, save for Persis Dewy's honest minutes which her righteous soul could not help couching in caustic language, especially the part about the great commission and the suggestion that it be rewritten. Then the meeting came to attention and the president turned a honey-sweet look toward the Old Guard.

"Now, ladies," she said, especially addressing the former members who were grouped close together today, "I believe the first thing on the docket is to inquire whether there is any report from our objectors of last week. Mrs. Dunlap, you were the first one to object to our new plans. Can you tell us whether anything has been done about raising the money to send out a missionary from the church?"

Mrs. Dunlap arose with almost regal bearing and answered quietly, "It *has*, Madam President."

"It *has!*" stared the president. "What has been done, Mrs. Dunlap?"

"The money has been *raised*, Madam President!"

"It—*has* been raised?" asked the president in astonishment. "How much, Mrs. Dunlap?" There was a note of doubt in the president's voice.

"The entire amount, Madam President, *and fifty dollars over*," said Mrs. Dunlap, trying to keep the note of triumph out of her voice and sensing the tense stillness that hovered over the room.

"You mean, I suppose, you have secured *pledges* to that amount?"

"No, Madam President! We have *the cash.*"

The air was fairly electric.

"May I ask," said the president after a second's hesitation, her voice taking on an accusatory tone, "just what *influence* you used to secure this sum in such a short time in these days of depression?"

"Yes, Madam President. We went to our heavenly Father, knowing that the silver and the gold are all his, and the cattle upon a thousand hills. We asked him and he sent it to us. The main part of it he sent to us through the father of the little child whom our Mary Lee taught how to die, but each of our members has had a part. And we have not asked a soul for a cent, not anyone but our heavenly Father."

The president gripped the desk and seemed to be bewildered at first, but rallied as she saw Mrs. Kingdon rise to the situation.

"Madam President," said Mrs. Kingdon grimly, "I think these good women should be commended for getting together so much money, *no matter how* they did it! And now I think we should try to get together with them and combine our forces. You see I have been inquiring and I find that it will take quite a little more to send Miss Melville to India than it would some less prepared young woman, and this sum that these good women have got together will nicely fill out our budget so that we can go before the board and not be ashamed. And now I feel that we should make it quite plain to these good friends who did not seem to understand last time, just what a wonderful young woman we are sending, and how well she will fit into a reconstructed program of missions."

Suddenly Mrs. Dunlap arose.

"I just want to make the ladies understand very plainly about this," she said in a kind but firm tone. "This money was raised to send *Miss Mary Lee* to India, and will not be available to send any other person. Neither will it be diverted to any other cause than the one originally planned by our society and Mrs. Bonner."

Then arose quite a babel, beginning with gentle persuasion, running the gamut of laughter, sarcasm, sneers, and scorn as the time sped away, and the new president was not getting anywhere with her argument.

At last Mrs. Searle drew herself to her full dainty height and said that unless this thing could be arranged amicably she would be obliged to resign. But lo and behold, when the matter came to a vote the Old Guard and their followers outnumbered the new contingent by enough to make a quorum, and the new president found herself confounded.

She made as graceful a retirement speech as she could frame on the spur of the moment, and lightly, with a haughty little smile, came down from the platform and went out of the room, followed by her satellites, Mrs. Kingdon bringing up the rear.

As she reached the hall door Mrs. Kingdon turned and looked back and spoke in a harsh voice.

"Ladies, you will find that you have made a very grave mistake, but I just want to say in leaving that you have convinced me more firmly than ever that the most dangerous thing we can do for the poor heathen lands is to introduce any more such narrow, bigoted views as we have seen exhibited here today! Good-bye, and I hope you find out before it is too late how foolish you have been, for this society will surely be on the rocks before the year is out!"

"Yes, on the rock Christ Jesus!" answered Mrs. Dunlap joyously.

"Praise the Lord!" said the little woman whose Johnny was in heaven by the grace of the Lord Jesus and the witness of one Mary Lee.

There was an automobile accident that night, and Mrs. Lansing Searle was thrown over an embankment and terribly injured. She lay a broken thing among silken coverings, and stared death in the face. She had made them tell her that she was going to die, that she had but a few hours to live. No one will ever know all that passed through her anguished mind in those hours. But at last there came the vision of the plain little timid woman in the missionary meeting and her story of the little boy who had been afraid to die. And then that startling sentence, "*You* might have to die someday, too, Mrs. President!" And Mrs. Lansing Searle remembered Mary Lee and her sweet, sure faith.

It was long past midnight when they sent for Mary Lee, sent a great limousine to bring her, and begged that she would hasten, for the time was short.

Mary Lee entered the great mansion where the Lansing Searles lived, and trod the velvet stairs, her heart crying out for the right word to give this passing soul. Her face was filled with the look she would wear someday when she pointed other sinners in India to the cross of Christ, her eyes seeing not the luxury about her, but only looking to Christ for help.

She knelt by the dying woman and took her soft white hand that already had the chill of death creeping over it.

"I've got to die and I don't know God!" wailed the woman who had been so self-sufficient.

"But God knows you," said Mary Lee gently. "He's always known you and loved you. He sent his Son to bear the penalty of your sins so that you might go home to him without a spot or blemish or any such thing."

"Oh, I've got to meet God, any minute!" moaned the weak, shrill voice. "And he knows what my heart has been toward him! I'm afraid!" She wailed agonizingly.

Gently the sweet tones answered: "It's not that we loved him, dear friend, for we didn't, but that he loved us! While we were yet sinners Christ died for us!"

Tortured eyes looked out between bandages, wonderingly.

"Oh, I'm a sinner, a great sinner. I know it now." Her voice grew stronger with earnestness. "It's not murder and stealing and lying that make one a sinner. It's just not wanting God in your heart. It's wanting your own way—*that* is unforgivable!" Again her voice broke in a sob.

"No, that is already forgiven, too. Listen! 'All we like sheep have gone astray, we have turned every one to his own way, and the Lord hath laid on him'— on his Son Jesus Christ—'the iniquity of us all.' Dear Mrs. Searle, if you put your trust in that fact, that God has done that for you, you need have no fear, for he says, 'Your sins will I remember *no more*.' You are accepted by God in his Son. You are just as dear as his own Son to him. How he will welcome you to his arms!"

"But won't I have to be judged for my sins?"

"No, listen! These are Jesus' own words: 'Verily, verily, I say unto you, he that heareth my word, and believeth on him that sent me, hath everlasting life, and shall not come into condemnation; but is passed from death unto life.' If you have heard the word of Christ and believed what he says, you are saved. Do you believe?"

"Oh, I have to believe. I didn't think it was so but now I see it. It is different when you come to die."

"Well then, dear, don't you see the question of a believer's sins was settled once for all on the cross when our Lord Jesus Christ received in his own breast the judgment that was our due? The believer cannot come into judgment for the reason that Christ was judged in our stead."

"But don't I have to do anything?"

"Just believe. Look! If I said I wanted to give you this little Testament, what would you have to do to get it? See, I am holding it out to you."

"Why, take it."

"Then will you take his salvation?"

"Oh, I will. *I must*. There is nothing else!"

"Well, then, let us tell him so," said Mary Lee.

So she led the dying woman straight into the presence of her Savior on the words of prayer, introduced her and handed her over into his loving care like a lost, frightened guest who had wandered away from the mansion to which she had been invited, like an alienated child from the Father's home. Pleading the claim of God's great promises, pleading the death of Christ upon the cross, pleading his shed blood, she brought her beyond the shadow of a doubt into safety and security.

Mary Lee's voice broke in a joyous sob, and as she opened her eyes she saw slow tears steal from the closed eyes of the sufferer and a light of peace spread over her face.

"Oh, it's true!" cried the dying woman. "Why didn't I see it before? But I was too full of myself to listen. Jesus! *My* Savior! He *is* my *Savior!*"

"Isn't it blessed," thought Mary Lee, as she watched the look of peace growing deeper, "that it doesn't take time to know God!"

Then she bent lower to hear the faint whisper that came from the dying lips. Those lips that but a few short days before had called the Bible an antiquated book were now asking: "What was that you said, Mary Lee—at the meeting? 'None other name'?"

Mary Lee quoted solemnly: "There is none other name under heaven given among men whereby we must be saved."

"Yes—that's it! Mary Lee, you tell those women —tell them I was *mistaken!* Tell them—there is no *other name!*"

Her voice trailed off into silence and Mary Lee thought she was gone, but suddenly she roused again and started up from her pillow, groping out as if she could no longer see: "Mary Lee! Mary Lee!" she cried. "Where are you? Mary Lee, you go to India and—*preach the gospel!*"